DEAD MAN'S ORBIT

Jupiter seemed to fill half the sky now, and they were heading straight toward its edge.

"Sheer off!" Tod said sharply.

Jerry shook his head. "I'm going into a braking orbit to save time."

"You're crazy. It's been tried, and Jupiter has three of the best pilots and a crew down there because Jim Thorpe tried it back in the early days when he was drunk. A lot of fool writers claim it has been done, but I never heard of the guy who did it."

"But—"

"But nothing. That's why they call it Dead Man's Orbit. Sheer off!"

The fear in Tod's voice was genuine. Jerry looked down at the planet and felt his face tighten as horror began to creep through him.

"Tod, I can't sheer off. We're too close. . . ."

Rocket Jockey

Lester del Rey

A Del Rey Book

BALLANTINE BOOKS • NEW YORK

A Del Rey Book
Published by Ballantine Books

Library of Congress Catalog Card Number: 52-8972

ISBN 0-345-30655-4

Manufactured in the United States of America

First Ballantine Books Edition: August 1978
Second Printing: October 1982

Cover art by David B. Mattingly

CONTENTS

CHAPTER 1 /

Rockets Away!

ONLY FOUR HOURS were left before the eighteenth Armstrong Classic would begin, and the two-mile concrete circle of the rocket launching site was a madhouse of last-minute activity. Ships and men from all the planets filled it, together with the hordes of reporters and fuel engineers. The air was thick with the smells of burning oil and ozone from the welders.

After the qualifying run to the Moon, there would be only one ship allowed for each planet, but now even Mercury had three entries, while Mars and Earth each had twelve. Soft-spoken, smiling Venusans in oil-stained nylon brushed shoulders with narrow-eyed, suspicious Callistans. Laughing Merculians bumped into slim, leather-clad Europans. But even in the confusion, Earthmen and Martians avoided each other.

Mars had won the last three Classics by what Earth considered unfair trickery, and there was bitter feeling between the two planets. Earlier, there had been fighting when they met, but now the Classic Police, selected from all the planets, had separated them, and everything was peaceful on the surface. However, even now, the police watched with careful eyes, and hands close to their heavy "peace sticks."

The Martian guard at the receiving platform still wore his native hard-leather costume—tight pants and a jacket with a hood attached—but the gold arm band showed he was one of the police. He watched the helicopter settle, and his stern eyes narrowed as a young Earthman got out and waved the driver away.

"Hold it!" the guard ordered crisply, but the taxi was already taking off. The Martian's hand dropped to the handle of his stick as he marched toward the boy. "No school passes today—"

Then he halted as the young man turned to face him. Jerry Blaine was wearing the green uniform and visored cap of a Space Institute Midshipman, but the gold buttons and stripes had been hastily ripped off.

He pulled a metal pass from the pocket of his wrinkled jacket and handed it over. "No school," he said, and there was bitterness in his voice. "My brother's got a ship entered—the *Last Hope.*"

The guard studied the pass doubtfully, hard, black eyes moving from the boy's carrot-red hair down the slim, short figure and back to the freckled face and blue eyes that stared out from behind glasses. At seventeen, Jerry looked like a bookish, unimportant person, not suitable for Space Institute, let alone a crewman on a racing rocket. It took time to notice the firm lips, the square jaw, and the deep tan that could come only from years in space.

"Okay," the guard said reluctantly, handing back the pass. "Pit 17, left." Then his lips drew back in a thin, sharp smile. "So Earth's going to beat us with infants this year, eh?"

Jerry saw an Earthguard moving forward quickly to back him up in case of trouble, and shook his head. He wanted no part of any quarrel. The Classic had caused too much ill will already. He moved away from the receiving platform and headed down the path the guard had indicated.

The heat of the July sun was worse here than it had

been in Chicago, and the shining walls of the ships, half-buried in the launching pits, reflected it back and forth. A blast of hot gases leaped up from one of the pits as a Venusan ship blew a test blast, lifting ten feet from the floor of the pit.

His brother Dick must be insane, he thought. He was doubly sure of it as he came in sight of the little *Last Hope,* with its space-worn hull and squat, ugly lines. Only a crazy man would want to race that against the trim, custom-built ships in the pits around, even if he wasn't already out of his mind to join the race in the first place. The ship had been built to mine the metal asteroids between Mars and Jupiter, not for racing, and it looked like a workhorse among thoroughbreds.

Then his eyes spotted the tall, graceful figure of his brother running toward him. Jerry broke into a run himself, and the bitter thoughts disappeared under a flood of his old love and admiration.

"Jerry, you old space flea!" Dick's deep voice was warm in his ears, and one of the big hands was grabbing his while the other pounded on his back. Then Dick drew back, studying him fondly. "Kid, you look like a million. You've grown two inches this last year!"

Dick looked good too. He was nine years older than Jerry, and years of work among the asteroids had made his skin tan to the deep brown only space could give. His black hair and gray eyes went well with it, and his figure was something that most professional athletes envied at first sight. Even the dirty coveralls couldn't hide that, nor the oil on his face conceal his good looks.

Then he sobered. "You're late, kid. I thought you'd be here early this morning. Wait'll you see what we've done to the old *Last Hope*—and what we still have to do. Boy, we need you, if we're going to be ready for blast-off by five-thirty!"

"I wired you I wasn't coming," Jerry told him.

"I know, but I figured you'd change your mind. I talked with Commodore Tenn last night. He told me you were in the middle of some examination, but that he knew you'd be glad to come!"

Jerry nodded bitterly. "Second year finals. I passed them, got my junior navigator's permit—and then Tenn called me in and kicked me out! He said—"

But he couldn't finish. The head of Space Institute had made it short and not at all sweet. Any boy who had a chance to compete for the glory of Earth and wouldn't take it wasn't good material for Space Institute. The Institute trained the best pilots and navigators in the Solar System, but it had to make men of them first. He was forced to discharge Midshipman Blaine from the Institute, and reinstatement would depend upon his conduct in the Armstrong Classic—in his proof that he was a man, as his fine and daring brother was a man. Navigator-Trainee Blaine would proceed at once to his room, remove his insignia, and report to his brother . . .

There had been no use in protesting that he'd spent long years with Dick's help studying and working to pass the entrance examinations, or that it had been Dick's dream, as well as his, that he should become a navigator-captain on one of the great luxury liners that sped between the planets. He was no longer sure that it was Dick's idea, any more.

He stared at his brother, expecting shock and surprise. But Dick only frowned, and turned his eyes away. "Tough luck, kid. But we'd better get back to work. We're behind—"

"Dick!" Jerry caught his arm. "Dick, did *you* ask old Tenn to sack me?"

He expected hot denial, and was ready to apologize for the suspicion that had hit him suddenly. But Dick turned his eyes away, frowning. His voice was uneasy. "Not exactly, Jerry. I thought you'd want to come along. We always brought each other good luck, together. Like the time I first took you along on my old space scooter, and you spotted the platinum asteroid."

"Like the time you helped me bone up for entrance exams when we *both* wanted me to be a first-license navigator!" Jerry reminded him sharply. "Like the way we used to talk things over together before we did anything!"

Dick winced and slowly turned to face the other. "Okay, Jerry. Okay, you don't think I'm much of a brother now. But I didn't have time—I only convinced Sun Fuels to back me three weeks ago. We went crazy rebuilding the old *Last Hope*—I just managed to jump her here from California in time to enter. And now, when we're up against deadline, the engineers Sun was sending from Luna Center blew a tube and can't get here in time. Look, kid, I *need* you!"

Jerry met Dick's eyes and saw that his brother meant it. He straightened his shoulders slowly, swallowed the bitterness that had filled his mind, and stuck out his hand again.

"Dick, why didn't you put it that way in the first place?"

Suddenly, things were all right between them again, as they had always been since their parents had been killed in the explosion, and Dick had turned asteroid prospector to keep them going. They came to Pit 17, and Jerry began running up the rope ladder after his brother, into the control room of the *Last Hope*.

Jerry gasped. Outside, the ship had seemed the same—almost as wide at the base as it was high, with a single huge rocket tube below, and a blunt, rounded tip. The broad steering vanes that looked almost like wings had been trimmed down a little, since there would be little maneuvering in atmospheres. But otherwise, no change had showed.

Inside, it was a different ship. The heavy braces and beams that made it strong enough to grab onto a small asteroid and move it had been removed. Slender struts replaced them. The control room, at the tip, was smaller than ever, barely big enough for two men. Then the center rail that served as a ladder from level to level led down to the combination workroom and living quarters. The big mining machines were gone. Three tiny cabins, a galley, a general room, and a tiny repair shop opened from the central shaft.

Below that had been freight space. Now it was filled with a level of food, air-restoring machinery, and water-recovery plants. Most of it, though, was now turned into space for the big fuel tanks that would be needed. And finally, where the old power equipment and rocket-mixing chambers had been, everything was new, compact, and confusing.

The whole interior had obviously been ripped out and replaced to fit the ship for the Classic.

A cry came up to them as they slid down toward the engines, and Jerry found that there was still one familiar thing.

"Knew you'd come, Jerry," old Tod MacLane said, with a touch of a smile on his wrinkled face. Then the smile clicked off, and the engineer was himself again, a gnarled, wizened little monkey of a man. His handlebar mustache had grown longer and grayer, and his eyes seemed to have sunk deeper into his head, but he was still the same otherwise. He'd been hired by Dick when they first bought the *Last Hope* after they'd found the platinum asteroid.

Jerry blinked. "Tod—you're not going . . ."

"Ain't I?" MacLane's face pinched up as he clenched his teeth down on a wad of Venus gum. The tarry stuff was a mild, harmless stimulant that had become popular on Venus during its settlement, and Tod was never without it. "Just try to stop me, Jerry Blaine! By dogs, I'm not sixty yet—but I'm too old to see them blasted Martians steal another classic from old Earth. This time, we gotta win. Here, you two dig in."

He'd gone back to a big valve as he spoke, and Dick had jumped down beside him. At first glance, everything seemed different, but Jerry's eyes soon showed him that most of the old system had been used as a pattern—and he knew that he'd be more useful to Dick than any regular engineer, unused to the compact plan of a meteor mining ship.

He reached instinctively four inches behind him and found the tool chest where it had always been. Without looking, he picked up a big wrench that fitted perfectly over a large hex nut and began working it around, as Tod and Dick together adjusted the motor-control valve that seemed to be the final stage of their overhaul work.

"Three-thirty," Tod muttered after what seemed only a few minutes of work. "Never make it. Gotta step it up, boys!"

The valve was the final control for feeding the fuel into the big rocket, and it had to be set exactly. Twice more they yanked it out, while Tod trimmed off a thin layer of metal. Jerry studied the maze of tubes that connected to it, and shook his head.

"You won't get enough power through that to win," he said at last. "Not unless you've got the best fuel ever made licked ten times!"

Dick grunted as he held the valve while Tod ground it away. In a properly equipped pit, there would have been power tools for this, but apparently there had been no time to install such things. "We've got twenty times better, kid. I'm using Dad's fuel!"

Jerry dropped the wrench, staring at him blankly. "You can't!"

That was what had killed his parents. He'd been only seven when they took off in a rented ship to test his father's new fuel, but he could still remember the flash of the explosion that had lighted space millions of miles back to Ceres where he and Dick had waited. There hadn't been even a trace of the ship left. It had been powerful enough—too powerful. He remembered now that Dick had sworn it wasn't the fault of the fuel, but nobody had agreed.

"I found the trouble," Dick said, as Tod finished. "I

located the man who'd repaired the ship Dad used—
and made him admit he'd soldered the tanks, instead of
welding them. Solder contains tin—and Dad's fuel used
tin as a catalyst to set it off! It didn't blow up coming
here from the coast."

"But that's only half an hour. What makes you think
it will be safe for days in space?"

Dick shrugged. "It will be. It has to be. I made a deal
with Sun Fuels, because they agreed that it must have
been the tin before. Now, once I win the Classic, they'll
go into all-out production. But right now, they've faith
enough to back me up, rebuild the ship, and pay the
entry."

Jerry saw it was useless to argue. They'd been trying
to convince him that Earth had to win this Classic. The
prestige of the whole Earth-based shipping had been
falling since Mars began to win, and Earth couldn't feed
five billion people without her shipping. Now she was
losing contracts to Mars—and only a victory could give
her hope again.

He could see some sense in it. But when he looked
around this hastily rebuilt mining ship and remembered
the sleek ships outside, he shook his head. Now, with
Dick counting on an unproved and dangerous fuel . . .

He shivered, just as Tod nodded. "Looks like we got
it, that time. Want me to turn her on, Dick?"

Dick nodded, while Jerry pondered. He'd meant to
help here until it was finished, and then refuse to go
with them. Maybe he was out at the Institute, but he
could get a job as midshipman on a freighter, and
maybe work his way up to navigator the hard way . . .
But now—could he back out? Could he let his brother
go off when it might mean death, and stay here . . .

Dick screamed.

A thin stream of black fuel was spurting out of the
valve, to stop as Tod's writhing muscles jerked the big
spanner wrench savagely around. But the damage was
done. Dick was moaning, his hands over his eyes, stag-

gering backward. Jerry jumped forward, easing his big brother toward a chest, while Tod made a convulsive leap up the railing toward the medical chest.

"I'm okay. Just got a touch," Dick was muttering, but his eyes were still closed. Jerry stared at him in horror, daring nothing until a proper sterile swab could be used. Then Tod was back, and he began working on Dick's eyes, while the man moaned softly.

Jerry moaned, too, when he saw the final result. The fuel came away, but it showed a reddened patch where it had hit, and Dick's eyes seemed filmed with a thin white coating. The medicine kit yielded a pain-killer that helped, but they could do nothing else.

"Get a doctor," Jerry told Tod.

Dick shook his head. "No time. I've got to take off." Then he stopped, and his face seemed to grow old. "Jerry, I'm blind! I can just see light, no more."

Above them, soft steps sounded, and a body began sliding down the railing. A pale-skinned man, dressed in the gaudy nylons of Venus, dropped beside them.

"Take-off whistle sounded, ten minutes more for you, Blaine," he said softly. "Thought maybe you wouldn't hear, being busy down here, so I—Blaine, are you sick?"

Dick stood up suddenly, grinning. "Thanks, friend. I'm all right—just got blinded for a minute by some fuel. Better get back to your own ship."

The Venusan nodded softly, a trace of worry in his friendly brown eyes. Then he turned. "Then good luck to one of us, and may we beat the Martians!"

He slipped up the rail again, like a cat, with the lithe grace of the men who had developed new ways on Venus. Dick grinned confidently and moved after him—to strike the rail with his head.

Jerry jumped after him, but Dick could see something by now. He caught the boy, and swung him around.

"No doctors, Jerry. We're taking off. I'll be all right

until we reach the Moon. You can get me a doctor then."

"Yeah," Tod said brusquely. "You young fool, who's gonna get us on the Moon?"

Jerry straightened his shoulders and moved toward the rail.

"I've got a junior-navigator's permit, Tod," he answered. "It's good for private ships in space. Help Dick into a gravity hammock, and then come on up."

He felt sweat on his palms as he began climbing the pole, but he didn't look back until he reached the little control room and threw himself down into the navigator's seat, before the big panel of instruments. He could hear Tod strapping his brother in, and he heard the engineer squeeze in beside him, but he didn't look around.

Outside, the big sirens began singing shrilly, while the clock on the dial moved second by second toward five-thirty. A flash of bright light flared outside, signaling *rockets away.*

Jerry hit the controls, and the *Last Hope* shuddered, lifted, and began screaming outward toward the Moon.

CHAPTER 2 /

Red Tape on Luna

FORTY-EIGHT SHIPS blasted savagely upward toward qualifying position at Luna Center. The first ship from each world would automatically be the one to represent its planet in the rest of the race, unless disqualified for some violation of the rules. That meant Jerry was competing only against the other ships from Earth, but eleven others against him was a serious enough threat.

He tried to spot the other Earth ships. Each ship had substances added to the fuel to color the exhaust—yellow for Mercury, white for Venus, blue for Earth, red for Mars, and shades of green for the four moons of Jupiter. He scanned the sky for blue streaks, and began pouring on power to break out ahead of the leader.

His body took on more apparent weight, sagging back into the seat, and his breathing became harder. The *Last Hope* seemed to groan faintly as the picture of Earth in the rear tele-panel shrank.

Tod shook his head in sour disapproval. "Let 'em go—they'll only try to fool you. We figure the best can do almost two gravities to the Moon, so you'd better beat it!"

Jerry blinked. A gravity was still based on the Earth's pull, which could accelerate a falling body thirty-two feet per second faster each second than the one before. Two gees meant reaching a speed of 157,000 miles per hour at the end of the first hour!

In the old days, ships had taken off at five gees or better—but they'd held it for only a few minutes, and then coasted. Now the rockets blasted all the way, accelerating and decelerating. At two gees, fuels produced more heat than thrust, and the tubes couldn't stand it.

"They're your tubes," he said finally, and reached for the knob, lifting the acceleration until the needle registered a full two gravities, and his body seemed to weigh twice what it should.

"Tubes are okay," Tod said. "Darn fuel breaks up funny—not much heat, all scat. I'm going down to see Dick."

He moved away, bent down under the thrust of the ship. Jerry tried to remember something about his father's fuel. It was supposed to come apart so that the forces inside the nuclei of the atoms built up a mutual repulsion, or something. There had to be some heat—otherwise, the turbines around the tube wouldn't have steam to drive the power for the rest of the ship. But Tod and Dick knew more than he could.

Now he could see no other ships. They were outside Earth's atmosphere, with the sky black and the stars tiny dots of searing light. He checked his course, and made sure on the little calculating machine that he was headed straight for where the Moon would be. Then he relaxed, with little to do until they reached midway, if he had figured correctly.

Something splashed against the quartz windows ahead of him—a fury of red light that almost blinded him before automatic shields snapped down. Another ship was ahead of him, driving its blast straight into the *Last Hope*.

He hit the buttons for the side rockets—tiny things buried near the base. The ship jerked sharply, and the tele-panels suddenly showed the bulk of a Martian ship slightly to the side.

It was no time for caution. He poured power into the big tube, and the *Last Hope* leaped forward on full five gees, driving the air out of his lungs and bringing red spots in front of his eyes. The Martian ship seemed to leap backward as his ship danced ahead. Then he cut power back to normal, and swung the ship in front of the Martian. Again, full power lashed out under his fingers for a second.

When he looked again, the Martian ship was swinging sideways and getting away as quickly as it could. They didn't want any more of the wild energy that had struck them from the rocket tube of the *Last Hope!*

Dick's big figure suddenly settled into the seat beside Jerry. "What happened? My sight's getting better, but I can't make out too much yet."

Jerry told him, while he began to set up corrections on the calculator to make up for the slight change in course and speed. Dick nodded.

"That's Mars. They must have used one ship deliberately, figuring it would sacrifice itself to take out the fastest Earth ship! Were the cameras on?"

Jerry looked, and groaned. No record had been made of it. They wouldn't be able to protest to the Classic Commission at Luna Center. "I forgot!"

"No matter." Dick's hand pressed his shoulder firmly, and there was approval in his voice. "You can't think of everything, kid. At least, you got us out of it— and we know we've got power behind us! Good work!"

There were no other mishaps. Jerry finished his calculations and corrected the course. An hour later, they were at midway point, and he swung the *Last Hope* around, using the steering tubes, and pointed the tail toward the Moon, to begin cutting down the speed for their eventual landing. He was beginning to get used to the heavy pressure of a constant two gees of acceleration, rapidly hardening back into the shape that years among the asteroids had given him.

Dick's eyes were improving. The redness around them had gone down, and the milky film over them was almost gone. The two of them watched the pock-marked face of the Moon fill the viewing panels, while Tod was down in the engine room, checking his precious machinery.

"Looks okay," he reported finally. " 'Course, we don't know how she'll stand up day after day, but she's purring like a kitten. D'ya hear from Center yet?"

Dick reached for the little radar-frequency radio and began calling the Moon, which was now close enough for their power to reach it. A minute later, he threw down the headphones and frowned.

"We're almost tied with Cap Amos and his ship! The fool must be burning out his tubes, figuring on replacing them at the Center shops. Look!"

He pointed, and Jerry swung his head. A few miles off, a glaring blue streak of flame showed against the black of space. Dick reached for the calculator, and Jerry cut off power, to let them go on at their present speed a bit farther. It would require a heavier braking thrust later, but they had to be first!

The tiny blue streak imitated their action, disappearing as Amos must have cut off his blast. They coasted on for ten minutes more, before Dick nodded reluctantly, and Jerry threw on power, raising the braking thrust to over two gees.

The streak came back on, seconds later.

Then flame blossomed suddenly! There was no sound in the airless space, but a great globe of searing white seemed to spring up where Amos' ship had been. The tubes had been crowded too hard and too long. Cap Amos and his ship were now only broken dust and heat!

Jerry felt sick. It wasn't worth it. Every ten years, good men and ships went out on this crazy Classic—

and many of them never came back. Now, in trying to beat the other ship, he'd helped to kill men against whom he had no ill will at all!

"He knew what he was risking," Dick said, in a voice that held some of Jerry's own sickness. "Watch your landing."

The *Last Hope* was over Tycho Crater now, and Luna Center showed up in the tele-panels. It was a great dome of clear plastic, filled with tightly jammed buildings. Most of the Moon colony was underground, but even the surface construction looked imposing.

Dick was on the radio, taking instructions and passing them on to Jerry. It was the most ticklish part of the business, but years of dropping the ship onto wild asteroids had given him sureness which no junior-navigator should have. As the smaller dome beside the big one seemed to split into two sections, he dropped through it, cushioned the ship on the blast, and eased it down to the ground. There was only a faint jar as the clock hands reached the hour of eight, and the *Last Hope* finished the qualifying run, to win the right to represent Earth in the Classic.

Jerry dropped his sweating hands from the controls, and turned to Dick. "Now we're getting you to a doctor."

Dick pointed to the mob pouring out of the big dome into the section around them, where the landing dome was again sealed and pumped full of air. "One's coming, kid. They automatically test us and publish the results after this run. And I don't mind admitting, I can use a little sedative."

Jerry stood up, and then gasped. Even in the weak gravity of the Moon, his legs were trembling with reaction until he could hardly stand. He slumped back to the seat as Tod came bustling through and went out to haggle the ground crews into refueling the *Last Hope* in less time than possible. The gray-haired little engineer seemed to be completely nerveless, but Jerry knew he wasn't. Praise be, he wouldn't have to make the full run as navigator-pilot!

In two hours, the *Last Hope* was refueled and ready to take off for Mars. Dick had been examined and pronounced fit, and Jerry was back to normal. They came out of the ship together to sign the papers for official scoring, and headed toward the Commission building in the main dome.

Jerry had been to the Moon before, but it had been years ago. He saw the Observatory dome, where the big 300-inch telescope still dominated the whole Center, and stared over the city. It hadn't changed—Luna Center was a fixed colony, serving the few mines and the laboratories, but completely dependent on Earth for its food, as it had always been. There were miners in their space suits, just in from outside the dome, scientists, and administrators. But there was none of the normal bustle and life of a real colony. It was still just a little artificially maintained bubble of life in a world that could never be of any great use, now that men had reached the planets.

They broke into the Commission office to find a milling mob around the three Commissioners. Earth representatives were shouting wildly, and Martians were standing in a cluster, with stern faces, grimly insistent.

The sounds quieted as Dick approached the big desk. "All ready for take-off clearance when we get official status," he reported.

The big man who was the Commissioner from Earth shook his head slowly. "Mars has protested, Blaine! They maintain that you could have not piloted the *Last Hope,* since a medical report indicates your eyesight was temporarily destroyed by an accident prior to Earth take-off. I've seen the report, and I'm forced to admit they have a point."

The babble of voices struck up again, the Martians glaring at all the Earthmen, with thin smiles of satisfaction on their faces.

"My brother piloted," Dick admitted. "He's qualified for the Moon run, and he's listed as a crew member, if you'll check the lists."

"But he isn't qualified for full interplanet runs. And the rules state that the pilot making the qualifying run must at all times throughout the course of the race be in command, both in authority and in ship control, through the entire event! We can't certify you for the Classic, Richard Blaine!" The Martian commissioner showed no emotions, but his decision was voiced with complete finality.

"Why, you dirty bunch of canal flowers!" Tod Mac-Lane's agonized cry rang from the back of the room, and the little man came boiling forward.

Jerry reached for him, but it was Dick's big arm that stopped the engineer.

Dick faced the Commissioners. "Then I'm demanding emergency owner qualifying tests," he stated, and his voice showed that he was forcing the calmness his words held. In spite of the rules, it had been customary for any crew member to pilot during illness or other emergency, and Mars was simply trying to make trouble again, as the planet always did.

The Earth Commissioner lifted the rules, and found the passage. "In the absence of a qualified pilot, the owner of a ship shall have the right to request any substitute he shall deem fit to apply for emergency qualifying tests, and the Commission shall then supervise such tests. In the event of satisfactory performance in such tests, the Commission shall grant to such emergency substitute full status as pilot for the course of the race." He lifted his eyebrows. "But that applies only to the start of the race."

"And you'll find that another rule states that 'after the qualifying event, the ships shall start from their Moon bases,'" Dick said. "That means the start of the race is from here, not from Earth. We've only qualified—we haven't started."

The Martian Commissioner started to protest, but the Venusan Commissioner smiled suddenly, and conferred briefly with his colleague from earth. "Permission for emergency pilot tests granted," he said softly. The Martian frowned, but nodded reluctantly. "Name your substitute."

Dick pointed to Jerry silently. Then, he grinned. "Give me a minute with my brother, gentlemen."

In the little room that had been pointed out to them, Jerry stared from Tod to Dick and back, shaking his head. "Even if I could pass, Dick, it isn't worth it. You'd never have a chance. No, I won't do it. Let someone else run for Earth. You've got your work, and I can do a lot better getting an honest job, instead of wasting time and risking our lives on a forlorn hope. No!"

Dick started to answer, then shrugged. But Tod hopped from his chair and bounced in front of Jerry, shaking a small, hairy fist under the boy's nose.

"You ungrateful whelp! Dick spent years working the asteroids for you, so you could go off to that sissy school—and now you pull this!" He spat out his Venus gum, his face turning brick red. "Every cent Dick has is in this race, and you go chicken! The asteroid—pfui! It's played out! I'm not going—" His words chopped off as Dick pulled him back.

Jerry swung to his brother. "Is it true, Dick?"

"It's true," the big man admitted reluctantly. "The asteroid wasn't as rich as we thought—the vein ended a year ago, and I've been freighting cargo for others, until Sun Fuels agreed to back me. I suppose that's why Tenn kicked you out of the Institute—I was behind on the payments. Sorry, kid!"

Jerry stared at the floor, realizing that he should have guessed. But he'd thought the platinum asteroid was solid ore and would last forever.

"Thanks, Tod," he said, at last. "We'd better get in

and start in on the tests. They'll take too much time, even if I can pass them."

With the Martians to watch, he knew they would be tough. And as they stood there, there was the deep rumble through the floor that indicated a take-off. Already, some of the ships that had qualified were beginning the jump toward Mars.

CHAPTER 3 /

Mars—and Trouble

THE TESTS were worse than Jerry had thought. He made landings and take-offs, flew the ship down narrow passes of imaginary obstacles, calculated orbits, and did everything that the Martian observer appointed by the Commission could get the Venusan observer to permit. Between runs, he was forced to answer all the questions that a first-class pilot and a first-class navigator might find on his tests. Some of those, of course, he failed.

But it was his asteroid experience that pulled him through; no trickier training ground existed than threading a ship through the crazy little hunks of rocks that circled the sun between Mars and Jupiter, and Jerry had helped Dick there since he was ten.

The final test was the one that even the most experienced pilots might dread—bringing the ship in, holding it up, and then landing on a tilted surface, without using his steering tubes.

For twelve solid hours, it continued. And at last, even the Martian nodded, and stamped approval on his test. There was no way of failing him. The Commissioner from Earth gave him his certification.

"You've passed—you slipped through by the skin of your teeth, young man, and some of your knowledge leaves a lot to be desired. But you know how to handle a ship. Good luck!"

Dick clapped him on the back, while Tod grinned grudging approval. Then they put him into his hammock to catch a little rest while the ship was again refueled with supplies Sun Fuels had rushed up by fast freighter from Earth.

It was two o'clock Thursday afternoon when they woke him for the take-off. They'd spent eighteen hours on the Moon, when they had expected to leave two hours after the qualifying landing. That left sixteen hours to be made up, and meant that all the other seven ships were well on their way. The Commission had refused Dick's request that time spent in the tests shouldn't be counted as racing time.

He was still tired, but he felt better as he saw that the damage to Dick's eyes seemed to be gone. "How's the seeing?"

"Fine, Captain," Dick answered. "We're ready."

It hit him then—the sole responsibility from now on would be his. Legally, Dick couldn't make decisions, since Dick was only the crewman Jerry had been—and Jerry was official pilot.

He glanced down at his crumpled uniform. Then his eyes went back to the field, where the all-clear signal was going up as the top of the little dome split for him to leave.

"Two gravities all the way, if we're to make up time," he decided, and was grateful for Dick's approving nod.

He glanced over Dick's calculations for the course, initialed them, and set the controls. His hand found the buttons, and the *Last Hope* lifted, with the prayers of all Earth behind it.

The pressure came on, sickening after the Moon's light gravity. Jerry swallowed, forcing himself to steady down. In the rear tele-panel, the Moon began to shrink, while the speed built up. Mars was not in the most favorable position, and the trip would cover some seventy million miles. With a steady two gees of acceleration, the *Last Hope* would be speeding along at nearly four million miles an hour by the time they reached midway and began to slow her.

But half an hour out from the Moon, there was nothing left to do but switch on the automatic controls and wait.

Dick pulled out the course sheets. Each pilot was free to choose his own course, provided he touched on all the inhabited worlds before returning to Earth. Figuring out the best way meant careful calculation of where each planet would be at the end of a run.

"Mars, of course," Dick said. "Some will swing down to Venus then, and some will head out to Jupiter. We'll try for Jupiter. The four Jovian worlds around the big fellow will have to be hit according to when we arrive. I'd figured it out that we hit Io, Ganymede, Europa and Callisto, in that order. Then Venus, Mercury, and back to Earth. It's based on a little less than nineteen days for the trip!"

"But the record is twenty-six days!" Jerry checked the figures and accelerations used, but it still seemed incredible.

"Records are always broken—that's the idea of the Classic."

Jerry estimated quickly. "We can make up better than four hours getting to Mars. That leaves about fifteen to make up on the Jupiter run. At full two gees we should be able to do it. Okay."

He initialed it, feeling foolish as he realized that he was in a position where his little knowledge had to be put against the years of experience Dick had.

Then they went on regular schedule, one sleeping while the other two watched. Jerry was awake again at midway, and he turned the ship on its side tubes. In empty space, with nothing around them, they couldn't use the vanes that would steer them in atmosphere. Even the cartoonists had finally given up the idea that space ships could move in long curves that would change their direction without losing speed. An airplane could, but a space ship had to build up speed and then turn over painfully to work just as hard killing that speed.

Turning was a matter of giving the ship a side thrust, letting it swing through 180°, and then exactly counterbalancing the first thrust. It was tricky, and frequently a number of small blasts were needed, slowly correcting errors.

Now they were falling toward Mars, while the hours ticked on. The new calculations called for forty-three and a half hours from the Moon to the fourth planet. And they were right on schedule.

This time, as they drew near the reddish surface, there was an atmosphere to help. Mars was an old world, and there was only a trace of air there; the planet had been too small to hold more than traces. But at rocket speed, even that little was enough for the steering vanes to shape their course. They came down at a long slant that slowed them against atmospheric friction, and waited until they were over the city of Eros, in the big section known as the Mare Cimmerium, before they began dropping downward on the thrust of the rockets.

Eros had one of the biggest rocket ports in the Solar System, since its ships had been increasing in commerce ever since Mars began to win the Classics. The landing space for the *Last Hope* was clearly marked, and there were no other racing ships there. The others had already landed and taken off again!

"Way at the end of the field!" Dick said bitterly. "We drew our positions by lot, but Mars always wins, and Earth loses! Now we've got the whole field to cover when we bring up fuel and supplies from the sheds over there."

The ship dropped down smoothly onto the field. It was a bit rougher this time, as Jerry was less familiar with landing where gravity was stronger than on the asteroids or the Moon. Mars was over a third as strong as Earth. He made it well enough, though, and entered the official time. Right on the new schedule! It was 9:30 in the morning, Saturday, by Earth time. As pilot, he climbed down to the portable receiving station the Martians had brought up, and got into a Mars suit, to take his papers to the local office of the Commission. Tod and Dick would supervise loading.

The Mars suit was an airtight plastic coverall with a light transparent helmet, something like a flimsy space suit. It had a little motor device behind the head that compressed the local air until it was heavy enough for breathing.

He had never been to Eros, but he'd landed on Mars with Dick before, and he was used to the suit.

The field was at the outskirts of the city, and he had a good look at Mars as the little taxi drew toward the city proper. No helicopters or planes could operate in the thin air, but the flat sandy wastes were an ever-present road for the caterpillar-tracked little cars.

Nearly all of Mars was a reddish, sandy desert. During some seasons, the wastes were covered with a thin, greenish growth of cactus-plants, but there was neither a mountain nor a sea on the whole surface. Water was so scarce that only delicate tests could reveal traces of it, and the cities baked their own moisture out of elements in the soil.

The canals were still a mystery. They were as sandy and flat as the rest of the planet, but great twenty-mile-wide strips that ran in long straight lines for thousands of miles were of a sand that differed in color. Plants seemed to grow somewhat thicker in the "canals," but there was no evidence that any animal life had ever existed on the little planet, half the size of Earth.

Jerry spotted one of the sandstorms off in the distance, a red haze in the air. But the thin wind was blowing away from Eros, and there would be no danger from that. The farms were uncovered in the thin light of the distant sun. Mars plants were cultivated now, supplied with a trickle of moisture more than they had ever known. The temperature was almost fifty degrees, but the sub-zero nights, even in summer, made growing Earth plants a matter for enclosed hydroponic gardens, where Earth conditions could be maintained artificially.

These farms at the outskirts of the city were the chief riches of Mars, since they produced strange foods and drugs that could be found nowhere else in the system.

Unlike most worlds, Mars did not enclose its cities any more. Each building was airtight, and the streets between were also enclosed, or buried under the surface. Men who went outside closed their helmets and breathed with the aid of the supercharges on the suits. Inside the cities, most of them still wore the suits with the helmets thrown back, though a few moved about in the hard-leather undergarments that were universal.

It was a stern, rough people who had developed here from the first colonies. Any race of humans who could wear those hard garments had to be tough, Jerry thought.

He found suspicion and dislike at the Commission office, but nothing to which he could object. They read his papers carefully and stamped them properly. He hadn't expected any courtesy, and he got none. Even the taxi driver had refused to speak to him.

Mars had no use for outsiders. The human population here reminded him of the grim, forbidding hillbillies he'd read about in the old books about Earth. They were scientifically advanced enough, but they were grim and unpleasant, with no use for fripperies or anything not completely practical.

He was glad to be back on the rocket field again, until he saw Dick's face. Then his heart dropped.

Dick shrugged unhappily. "Nothing we shouldn't have expected, kid. Nobody here knows anything about our fuel!"

"But we have to have fuel—we can't make the Jupiter run on quarter tanks!"

"That's right." Dick stared at the warehouses, where Tod was scurrying about frantically. "I've radioed Earth, and Sun Fuel says our fuel was delivered a week ago, landed and stacked in Number Six warehouse. They've got signed receipts. But all the men who did the storing seem to be sick! And nobody knows where it could have gone!"

Jerry grunted. He was finding out why Earthmen were so eager to beat Mars in the race—and why Mars had won the last three Classics. "Didn't we have someone here to watch it? Or is he sick, too?"

"He's sick, all right—with a busted head, in the hospital. I've claimed violation to the Commission; they say they'll investigate. But that will take weeks. All we can do now is investigate all the sheds. The Commission ordered them to let us do that."

There were over fifty of the big warehouses at the edge of the field. Dick, Tod and Jerry began searching, each taking one warehouse at a time. A stain on the floor showed where the fuel had been stored in Number Six—there was no mistaking the peculiar odor of the fuel, though the Martians claimed it was probably some other fuel shipment. But no other evidence could be seen.

The Martians offered no real trouble, but they gave no assistance, claiming all the men were busy with normal work. Doors were found locked, and it took time to find the keys. And a thousand delays were on every side of the three searchers. In the afternoon, about a dozen Earthmen who were on Mars on some business tried to join the search, but the Martians claimed and proved that the Commission had empowered only the crew of the *Last Hope* to investigate.

Night fell without results. The sky turned jet black, and millions of stars shone overhead. The air was so cold now that it began to draw the heat out of their bodies, even through the suits.

Jerry knew that they would eventually find where the Martians had mislaid the fuel—but it would take three more days, if they had to search every warehouse. He went back to the *Last Hope* for coffee, begrudging the time, but knowing he needed it.

From the control cabin, the city of Eros had taken on a strange beauty, with its lights forming a pattern against the black of the sky. Even the farms around added to it, since the plants had a dim phosphorescent gleam.

Then he dropped the cup onto the control board, and let out a cry. Dick came up quickly.

"Dick, don't those plants need ultraviolet light to shine? Isn't it fluorescence under u.v. lamps?"

Dick caught the idea at once. "You're right. The fuel does fluoresce! And we've got authority enough to make them pull down one of those lamps, or supply us with an ultraviolet lantern! Let's go."

It took time to get one of the lights. With the coming of night, the Martians had sent all but one watchman home, and he had to do a vast amount of telephoning to get permission. But they finally went back to the warehouse where the fuel had first been stored.

Under the rays of the light, invisible to the men, the spots of fuel on the floor broke into a greenish blaze of light. Hundreds of compounds did that under such light—but the color of this was unusual in its depth, and the brilliance was typical of nothing except their fuel.

Dick went ahead, throwing the light about to spot other traces. Any spilled fuel had been carefully wiped away, but some had sunk into the sand, and now it glowed back at them. They followed the marks slowly, often having to circle and scout for others, since sometimes fifty feet separated the traces.

The trail led them around to the back of the warehouses, and finally under the loading platform at the

rear of one they had already searched. There was a lit-
ter of debris there, but it came away, to reveal the
round drums of fuel!

The watchman shrugged. He muttered something
about it being very careless, but they'd been cleaning
the warehouses. He did put through the calls for loading
men, though.

And eventually, men began showing up. It was too
late for the Martians to stall now. Once the fuel was
located, they had to seem eager to get it on the *Last
Hope*, for fear that the Commission might disqualify
their world from the race.

It was midnight by ship's time when the fuel was
found, and one in the morning before the loading actually got under way. All the crew pitched in to help,
and the Martians seemed to work with a will. But the
distance across the field made it a slow operation, since
hauling the drums somehow took as much time as the
loading. Then the fuel had to be warmed before it
would pour—the bitter cold of Mars had made it con-
geal in the drums.

Jerry got on the phone and began calling the Commission representative. Calls must have gone through
from Luna Center, too, because the Martian lost no
time in coming out to certify their new departure time.

"If you'll sign a waiver of all claims against Mars for
this unfortunate delay," he suggested blandly. "Of
course, you don't have to. But we should check your
ship to make sure that you have no contraband drugs—
there's been smuggling to the Jovian worlds lately.
Seems to me a little mutual trust and friendship is better
than all this formality, though."

He held out the waiver together with the certificate.
Jerry started to throw it back at him, and thought better
of it. For a Martian, the man was smooth, but he probably could enforce the search. Jerry sighed, and accepted the proper certification.

From landing to take-off should have taken no more

than four hours, but it had actually used up over eighteen hours. The clock now indicated four in the morning, Sunday. They were now twenty-six hours behind their schedule.

It was cold comfort to realize that Mars' spies must have decided their ship was the most serious danger to Mars' victory. The twenty-six hours probably gave Mars more than enough margin to win—if nothing else came up.

After the trouble, though, Jerry was sure of one thing. He no longer considered the race unimportant—and even the money involved didn't matter.

Somehow, he had to beat Mars!

He caught the all-clear signal, and his fingers bit down savagely on the controls, rocketing the *Last Hope* up toward Jupiter. Two gees was all he could use safely, but he wasn't going to use less for even a second of the jump!

CHAPTER 4 /

Emergency Return

JUPITER, the largest planet in the system, lay over four hundred and eighty million miles away from the sun—three hundred and forty millions of miles beyond the orbit of Mars. But it was farther than that from the location of Mars now—the planets were scattered about, instead of lying in the straight line that would have made for the shortest possible course.

They would never touch the giant planet. It lay under thousands of miles of atmosphere—methane and ammonia, mostly—in a cold where liquid oxygen probably ran down cliffs of frozen carbon dioxide; in that atmosphere, the *Last Hope* would have been crushed flat at once. Even if not, it would have floated miles above the surface, since the gases were so dense that they were heavier for the same volume than the ship.

Instead, they would touch on the moons around Jupiter. Four of those moons were about the size of Earth's moon, or larger, and they rotated about the big planet at distances of from a quarter million to over a million miles.

Jerry looked at Dick's chart and saw that Dick had allowed a hundred and eight hours to reach Io, the inside moon. At full two gees, they could shave about ten hours off that, or a bit more. It wouldn't make up for all the time lost, but it would help. He doubted whether Mars could make it much before he did, and tried to renew his hope for success.

Dick hadn't given up. It was impossible to tell about Tod MacLane; the engineer fussed over the tubes and motors, grumbling and fuming to himself, while he chewed great wads of the Venus gum savagely. He was always willing to talk about the Martians, but he refused to say what he thought of their chances.

Jerry slept, and woke up stiff. The constant pressure of the acceleration had something to do with that, but he knew that it was his own nerves, more than anything else. He'd begun to forget about the Institute, and even the bitterness at the dirty trick fate had played on him was wearing away. Now, all he could think of was the need to beat Mars.

He saw that Dick seemed to be suffering from the same strain. His brother's face was tensed, and his words were abstracted, as if he only half-listened. Jerry caught him often with his head down over the charts.

"You all right, Dick?" he asked finally.

Dick nodded, getting up and heading back toward the little cabin where he slept. "I'm fine, kid. Just keep trying to push the ship along faster than she'll go. Feel like I could get out and run faster!"

It was an easily acquired feeling. Once away from the planets, there was nothing by which they could judge their speed. Their bodies grew used to the extra feeling of weight, which remained constant, and the stars were so far away that no movement of the ship mattered. A man could stand at the quartz ports in the control room, looking out for hours, and see no change. Mars had shrunk to a dot behind, and Jupiter was only a dot ahead—no change in size showed now.

It would have been better if they could have known how the other ships were doing, but wise pilots long before had found that it didn't pay to try to discover that.

You couldn't figure who was ahead when everybody was following a course of his own choosing, and trying to beat the ones who were on the same course with you was both futile and dangerous. All that could be done was to make the best possible time, and hope you were good enough.

Jerry finished his watch and went down to wake Dick. He was surprised to find the little cabin dark—usually, in space, men got into the habit of sleeping with lights on, so that they'd be ready in case of one of the rare collisions with a meteorite or other danger.

He found the bulb and screwed it in, but his ears noticed that something was wrong before the light came on. Dick's breathing was heavy, and he was moaning softly with every breath.

He was asleep, and Jerry saw by the bottle beside him that it was a drugged sleep. The left eye had swelled up, and was a patch of darker skin in his already tanned face. Even asleep, he was frowning in pain.

Jerry let out a yell for Tod down the central shaft, closing the little cabin door before he did so. Nevertheless, the sound woke Dick, and he sat up, grabbing his head as the sudden motion seemed to send new waves of pain lashing through him.

He tried to grin up at Jerry and the little engineer who came bounding to the door. But the effort wasn't successful. It looked like a grimace of agony.

"Just a headache, kid," he muttered. "I'll be all right. I can still see fine. Let me sleep an hour more, and I'll take over."

Tod took a close look at him. "Crazy! Every Blaine ever born was crazy, and you kids are the worst! Dick, you stop your dadburned lying and tell the truth!"

"It's an order, Dick," Jerry said, as he eased his brother back gently onto the hammock. "Official!"

He was on sure grounds there; one of the duties of a captain was to insure the health of his crew. Dick scowled for a second and reached for a cigarette. He'd made a joke of Jerry's being captain, as Jerry himself had treated it. It came as a jolt to him to realize that their positions really were changed. He blew out a slow cloud of smoke, and tried another grin, this time with more success.

"You're right, Captain." He indicated the pills, and pulled out a thermometer from behind them. "I've pulled a flop at treating myself. Okay, I've got two degrees of fever, and it feels worse. Light hurts my eyes— oh, I can see fine, but it doesn't feel good. The whole side of my face feels as if someone walked on it. And I'm up against everything they've told me a migraine headache is. It's getting worse too. But I'll last till we hit Io!"

Jerry met Tod's suddenly worried eyes, and lifted an eyebrow. The engineer jerked his thumb downward sharply. Jerry agreed.

Dick had guessed the meaning. He stared at them, starting to shake his head. Then he sank back on the hammock. "How far out are we?"

"Eighteen hours."

"Eighteen more to stop—thirty-six to get back . . . We'll lose seventy-two hours!"

Jerry reached up and unscrewed the bulb again. "So we lose it. You're confined to quarters, Dick. And officially, I'm still running the ship. We're heading back for Eros, unless the radio can get me the dope on how to treat you. Right?"

Dick shrugged helplessly, while Tod began wrapping a thin blanket around him. Jerry went up to the control room. He cut off the power of the big tube, leaving only a slight amount of thrust to give enough gravity so that Dick wouldn't be thrown from his cot.

Then he reached for the radio switch. He had little hope for it, but it had to be tried first. He began lining the little beam-antenna for Eros, and let the tubes warm up. Tod came in, so silently that Jerry didn't hear him until the gum popped loudly.

"Never make it," Tod said. "Too far to reach. Good set on Eros, but they can't do miracles. Wait a minute."

He was back half a minute later, with a big transformer in his hands. "You need power. You're working on the ship's normal 220 volts, boy—this'll give you double that. Overload the tubes, but maybe they'll take it. Darn fools! Told 'em they shoulda left the emergency overpower in, like we useta have. Now I gotta kill other stuff to make this work. Ugh! There."

The tubes glared hotly, and there was a rush in the phones. Jerry began calling Eros. He cut power for fifteen seconds, and threw the switch again. It would take over that time for the signal to reach Mars and return over the distance.

Then the rushing sound cut off, and a voice reached him, faintly, but clearly enough. "Mars Interplanet, Eros. We get you. Come in, *Last Hope*."

"Good man for a change," Todd muttered, as Jerry began sending details. "Sense enough not to waste time."

It took fifteen minutes of off-and-on conversation before the doctor on Mars could get the facts, check with Dick's medical examination on Luna Center, and make up his mind. But that was less than Jerry had expected.

"Fuel must be in the back of the eye, irritating the optic nerve—just a trace. It needs surgical draining. Whole system may be poisoned slightly. Better bring him back, Blaine." The voice hesitated, and then took on a curiously human tone for one of the usually terse, grim Martian humans. "And Blaine—our medical ethics are just as sound as any other planet's. It's an honest report, not an attempt to delay you. Get your brother back here!"

Jerry acknowledged, and cut off the power. He'd heard that the Martian doctors were the best in the system, but he knew nothing of their ethics. He didn't care.

He couldn't take chances. Tod was muttering, suspicious still, but he grimaced, reached for the controls, and began reversing the ship.

Now he could have used that impossible ability to make a sweeping turn in space. But the laws of nature didn't change to please him. It took fifteen minutes more to turn over, and then the ship began blasting back for Mars.

Dick grew slightly worse, and was delirious. Jerry sweated it out, occasionally snatching a little sleep. But the trip out that had seemed short, now seemed to be endless on the return leg.

He was surprised to find that space was cleared for him, and marked with a big red cross at the field—a position nearest the gate. He rode down on a wash of flame, but steadied, careful that no jar would wake Dick, who was sleeping fitfully. It was a perfect landing.

A man in white overalls and helmet with a caduceus emblem was running up the ladder before the ground could cool, and others were following with a sling. There was none of the cold, stern hostility they had found on Mars before.

The doctor pushed into the control room, and followed Jerry, tossing words at the young man as they slid down. "Doctor Jorgens, Blaine. I talked to you. We're all set at the hospital to operate at once. Doctor Paulson, the best surgeon on Mars. This the patient?"

He made a hasty examination, and quickly began working with a hypodermic. "This will make him feel better. I've got full emergency authority, straight from your Commission. If you need more fuel . . . I thought so. Gregg, get the ground men working on that fuel, and hook up the air hose."

One of the men with the sling went off, and the other internes began bundling Dick gently into the hammock part of the affair, while others were fastening it with hooks to the outside of the *Last Hope*.

"May I come?" Jerry asked.

The doctor nodded. "Expected you to. Your man can supervise here at the ship while they're fueling, and you won't waste time. All right, easy now!"

They lowered Dick gently, and a ground force carried him to the ambulance. Jerry dropped in beside the doctor, and they went screaming off across the sand toward the big hospital building. Dick slept quietly now.

Jerry never could remember much of the hospital, save that he found none of the coldness or hatred he had expected on Mars. The Martians might be the most tough-shelled and treacherous people of all the colonies, but they seemed to take medical emergencies with as much feeling as the courteous, kindly Venusans might. Maybe the dark days of early settlement, when disease and privation had killed so many, had given them that attitude. For a moment, the race was forgotten.

It was two hours later when Doctor Paulson, a slim, nervous man, came out. He smiled wearily, and nodded to Jerry. "It's drained. Lucky you got him back, or he'd have gone blind. Now, he'll be all right in a few weeks. Like to see him?"

Dick lay in bed, with his face in bandages. He was still under the anesthetic, but the lines on his face had smoothed out. There was nothing Jerry could do, except to try to thank the doctors, particularly Doctor Jorgens.

They shook it off, as a matter of course. "It's our business, Blaine. And don't worry about the expense— the Mars office of Sun Fuels has already offered to pay anything."

"Can I help in any way, though?"

"Get back and take off. He'll feel better when he comes to if he finds you're not wasting time, unless I'm wrong about that young man." Jorgens smiled. Some of the harshness of Mars mixed with the smile, but it was still the warm smile of an older man trying to comfort a younger. "The ambulance will take you back."

They headed back to the ship with the big blinkers

twisting on the ambulance. Sirens wouldn't work in the thin air of Mars.

At the ship, the loading was already finished, and Tod had been told the news about Dick, obviously. He stood in the control room as Jerry got ready for take-off, shaking his head.

"I still don't trust 'em, Jerry. They got some trick up their sleeve."

Jerry shrugged. It didn't matter. Probably Mars had been happy enough to know that he had to put back; they didn't need to pull tricks when bad luck was helping them along the way. The *Last Hope* seemed jinxed. Or perhaps the Martians really were as human under it all as their ancestors from Earth had been.

He cut on the big rocket, and they went up from Eros again, for the second time. It was Wednesday now, seven A.M. by Earth time. Before, they had been twenty-six hours behind. Now the trip out, the return, and the waiting had taken up seventy-five hours more. They were heading out finally on the second lap of the great race one hundred and one hours—more than four whole days—behind their schedule.

As soon as he could, Jerry threw the ship onto automatic control and began figuring out a new course. The old one had been prepared by Dick, who depended as much on habit as mathematics to locate the position of the big planet with the help of the star charts. Jerry had to sweat it out on the calculator. Jupiter moved in its orbit over eight miles every second, which meant that it was more than two million miles farther along than it had been when the other course was charted. This made a small change in angle—since Jupiter's orbit was so huge a circle—but everything still had to be refigured.

He was still rechecking, six hours out, though his new course had already been fed into the automatic pilot. The radio buzzed. Only the big station on Eros could have reached him at this distance, and he jerked for the phones.

Dick's voice reached him faintly, since there was only normal power in the set. "Hi, kid."

He shouted back, wondering whether he'd already missed the regulation identification or whether this was more medical cutting of red tape. He didn't care.

"Feeling fine now," Dick's words came, seconds later. "They gave me only a minute, so here it is. Don't worry, they're treating me fine. Sun Fuels shipped an Earth nurse up from their office, over at Marsburg. Glad you took off at once. I'm weak as a kitten, but the news bucked me up. Beat 'em, kid! Over to you!"

Jerry sent back the most cheerful words he could, not forgetting to tease Dick a little about the nurse; it wouldn't sound honest without that. Then the official radio operator came on with the proper formalities, and they signed off. Apparently the doctors were still keeping Dick under careful supervision, but it was good to know he was himself again.

Tod grinned more happily at the news, and shoved Jerry out of the control chair. "You're beat, kid. Go catch some shut-eye."

Jerry stumbled down the rail, and into his bunk. He hadn't known how tired he was. He'd been too busy worrying about the course and Dick to remember that it had been a long time since he'd had more than a touch of sleep.

Now his eyes were closed almost at once. But the number of hours already lost kept running through his head, and he couldn't sleep properly. They might make it all up, but only if there was no more trouble. And he had a feeling there'd be plenty of that.

He groaned suddenly. Trouble—and no Dick for advice. He was on his own now—pilot of a racing rocket, against the best pilots in the whole Solar System. And Dick was millions of miles away.

It was a long time before sleep came to him.

CHAPTER 5 /

Raw Space

JERRY felt better after the sleep. Under double gravity, a man had to sleep more and his food intake went up somewhat. Every movement required more work than it would under a normal weight—even blinking an eyelid took extra effort. It could become normal enough, in time, but the energy must be supplied somehow.

His muscles were toughening in nicely, though. In the asteroids, under the varying pulls of weak planetoid gravity and terrific ship acceleration, he'd grown adaptable, as well as far stronger than any normal boy on Earth. He didn't look it, but he could lift twice his own weight on Earth with one hand, and without seeming to strain.

It was for that reason that he'd been forbidden to join in any of the sports at Space Institute; Earth had a standing rule against deep-space men participating in sports, since no man who hadn't left the planet could compete with them.

He reached for his glasses, and then remembered that he'd left them in the control room. They changed his appearance. He studied his face in the tiny mirror as he washed up, and decided to leave them off. Contact lenses were better, but he'd gotten into the habit of wearing

39

glasses; on Earth he'd looked too old for his age before he began wearing them, due to the space tan and his experience with Dick. They'd given him a neutral age, along with the bookish look. Now, as captain of the ship, he'd do better to look as old as he could when he contacted other worlds.

He relieved Tod, and began checking his calculations again, using a group of instruments to plot his position by several of the important stars. As far as he could determine, they were where they should be, and ticking along nicely at a higher acceleration than had ever before been attempted as a steady grind. They were approaching three million miles an hour in speed, and going faster with every second. Before they turned over and began slowing again, they'd be close to a speed of eight million miles an hour. It would probably be the all-time record up to now, since high speed could be built up only on a long run, and most long runs were made at lower acceleration.

He went down to inspect the big tube and the engines. Everything seemed to be in good shape. The pyrometer that indicated the temperature of the tube was down in the green section, completely safe, and the turbine that operated off the tube heat was purring along, keeping the tiny, efficient little batteries charged.

If they made the trip successfully, there could no longer be any question but that his father had been right. The fuel was behaving perfectly. He could remember his father only dimly, but it still felt good to know that Blaine's reputation as a fuel engineer was to be vindicated.

Then the long trip began to drag on. They were too far out for word to reach him about Dick, but he felt sure that there was no real worry now. He began to draw up a map of the positions of the little moons around Jupiter, and to plot his course to use the smallest amount of time, according to their positions. It was a slow business of trial and error, where he had to calculate dozens of courses and choose the best. But it was here that he had the best chance to gain or lose time. Most of the pilots were poor navigators, and the ships had little machinery for calculation.

Jerry had the advantage of two years of the best possible schooling, on top of his years in space. Where many of the others would have their courses charted in advance at some observatory, he could figure his own. If they lost time anywhere, it would throw them off completely. He meant to take advantage of any such breaks.

It took up his time until Thursday changed to Friday. He rechecked his last calculations, and nodded with satisfaction. He'd clipped five hours off the time his first rough figures allowed—and still left time enough for refueling and normal delays.

He put it aside and glanced again at the clock. Two-thirty, Friday morning, not yet two days out from Mars, but at least farther than they had been when he'd turned back before. In another few hours, he'd turn over and start braking down.

Suddenly he lurched in the seat. The ship seemed to go weightless, and then to pick up more weight than ever. It ran on smoothly for a few minutes, and then bucked again. This time the bucking became regular.

He glanced at the radar screens, but there was no sign of any meteorite which might have cut on the automatic course-changing mechanism. That should have given an alarm, anyhow.

He grabbed for the phone, buzzing for Tod. The little engineer's voice came back sharply. "Don't know what, Jerry. But it's down here. Better shut her off. Those blamed Martians! Bet they did something while we got loaded!"

Jerry cut off the blast, letting the ship coast on at its present speed of slightly less than seven million miles an hour. Without the drive, he was completely weightless. His body tried to bounce out of the chair, thrown by the rebound of the cushions, but he caught himself in time.

He felt his hair suddenly stand on end and wave about as he moved. With no weight to hold it down, it soon separated into a fuzz all about his head. His clothes ballooned out. For a second, his stomach seemed to turn over. But he'd been weightless before, and he knew it was only temporary.

He pulled himself up carefully, drifted to the central shaft, and threw himself down it, using one hand on the rail to guide him. At the bottom, he doubled over in mid-air and landed on his feet, checking the rebound by grabbing the rail more firmly.

Tod was moving around busily, seemingly as happy without weight as a bird in the air. He might almost have been one. He moved from place to place by pushing against anything convenient and floating toward his goal, with unfailing good aim.

Now he was busily prying open a section of the tube, using long tools to handle the hot stuff. He felt in with probes and metal mirrors that had filters built into them to bring the glaring, white-hot metal down to visible level. The mirrors would work until they grew too warm, but he was careful to expose them as little as possible before withdrawing them.

"Well?" Jerry asked.

Tod nodded. "It's here, all right. Must have been something in the fuel. The jet's clogged, and it's cutting off the fuel feed. Got a big hunk of slag grown up over it. We'll have to scrape it off."

He probed in again, his eyes glittering as he inspected the damage. "Too far to reach from here. I told you the Martians weren't as milk-and-honey as they acted. Now, see? We gotta go outside."

Jerry shivered. Nothing worried a spaceman more than having to leave his ship and move about outside to repair it. The space suits were a big improvement over those of the old days. They were fairly light, and they carried enough air for about six to eight hours, and were able to keep the wearer comfortable under almost any conditions of heat or cold. But the old stories of slipping off and going sailing off into nowhere, to drift until death came of asphyxiation, were still too common.

"Nothing else we can do, Tod?"

"Nope—unless you want to soup up the radio and send out an SOS for a space tug to come and take you back."

"How long?" Jerry asked. Even without the danger of going outside, it would mean a loss of time. They'd continue drifting at their present speed, but there would be no way to increase it—and each minute counted.

Tod shrugged, and began gathering his tools together. Jerry went up to the control room, to make sure everything was cut off. He shut off the automatic meteor detector; men had been killed for forgetting that, when the detector located a rock in space and cut on the steering tubes for a few seconds.

In space, with no air to drag back on one, speed meant nothing. To a man walking on a ship going millions of miles an hour, the ship seemed to be standing still, because both man and ship had the same speed. But any change in speed would throw him off.

If a meteorite came along, it would be too bad. But those were rare. Jerry had automatically set the course to rise well above the plane of the ecliptic—the flat plane of the planets around the sun; there were millions of bits of rock in the asteroid belt between Mars and Jupiter, but by going upward a million miles or so, they avoided all those. And except in the belt, accidents from such things were too rare to worry about.

He began climbing into his space suit, adjusting it to fit him. He checked the air. The old automatic habits of a meteor miner came back to him without requiring thought, and Tod nodded approval. There was no radio installed in the suits, and no way they could talk, except by touching helmets together, or each touching helmets to the ship, which would then carry the sound.

Jerry had been on some of the smaller asteroids, little hunks of rock only a few hundred feet across, and didn't mind that. But when the locks of the ship opened, and he went out to see nothing at all near by except the ship, it was different. He hesitated, automatically feeling that he was falling into a bottomless cavern. He closed his eyes and swayed dizzily.

It lasted only a few seconds, before shame at himself overcame the feeling. But the helmet of Tod clicked against him. "It's all right, lad," the engineer said with surprising softness. "We all feel it. I don't cotton to the idea myself. Well, out we go."

The old man reached out for one of the small handgrips with which the ship was covered and pulled himself out of the lock. Jerry hesitated again, and then followed his action. They moved toward the rear of the ship a few feet, stopping to clamp the rope around their waists to a new handhold every half-dozen grips they traveled. It was slow work, but it paid to be safe. Without the rope, a single careless movement could throw them off into space. With the big rocket off until it could be cleaned, it would be impossible to rescue any man who drifted away.

They came to the big tube, finally. There Tod began clamping a series of short ropes to handholds in such a way that he would have a limited amount of movement, but wouldn't bounce away from the ship every time he used a tool. Jerry studied his example and did the same.

Here they could have used elastic ropes, but such things were useless in space; the absolute cold would slowly make them stiff and brittle. Even the silicone fabric ropes they used were safe for only a few hours, and their suits were usable for longer only because heat was supplied from inside.

Tod began unscrewing a big plug in the tube. He bent sideways to touch helmets with Jerry as he did so. "One advantage of using an old meteor mining ship, lad. They expect accidents on these things, and they fix it so we can get to the trouble. On those pretty little racing jobs, we'd be sunk. Darn that plug!"

The heat of the tube had made the plug swell just a bit differently from the tube, and it was stuck. Tod sprayed a jet of liquid oxygen from his suit on it. There was no sound of a hiss, but the plug turned with their next effort. They worked it out, until they could see the big hunk of slag that covered the nozzle of the tube.

"Hard as diamond, almost, I bet," Tod grumbled.

He was right. The heat had fused out the softer elements, leaving only something that might have been carborundum. They began picking at it with the long-handled tools, trying to chip it away. It was somewhat brittle, fortunately. A well-placed blow could knock off a chunk of it.

But it was slow, tedious work, and it would get worse as they began to reach the nozzle itself. There, they'd have to be careful not to cause damage to the functioning of the tube.

Jerry sweated inside the suit, while the tiny round spot that was the sun blazed through empty space at him, glaring through the filters of his helmet. He was wondering whether it had been the Martians again. He couldn't believe it; they'd seemed too genuinely concerned. And yet, all the evidence of previous races indicated they would try any treachery to win. It wasn't a sport to them, but a grim struggle to build up their trade, and they didn't care how they won, so long as they did win.

Maybe Earth had played unfair, once, he decided. Or maybe some of Earth's ships still would. And how would the Martians be received on Earth, if they stopped there for refueling? He'd seen bitter hatred in the eyes of Earthmen whenever the Martians made a move. Maybe the whole trouble was one that could be cured only by making commerce so easy that there would be no bitter struggle for survival, and everyone could afford to be friends. His father's fuel, with its tremendous power and low heat production, might be a partial answer.

The bell in his suit clanged, reminding him that he'd better renew his ropes and change to fresh oxygen tanks before his air ran low. He tapped Tod on the shoulder, and the older man nodded.

Again they threaded their way back, being even more careful this time, since their ropes might be more brittle than they should be.

This time, they brought files and rasps with them, since the slag was getting close to the nozzle. The worst of the hatred of being out in raw space was over now. But Jerry had too much respect for the emptiness around him to be careless.

He fastened down again, and began working with Tod, using a long hammer to knock off what he could. The slag was more brittle now that the tube was cooling, and they could get closer. But it was also harder than it had been when hot.

Slow bit by slow bit, the scrapers chewed it away, and the files began to smooth it down. It didn't have to be too smooth, but it had to be free of all traces of the slag to prevent another clump from forming.

"How hot is it?" Jerry asked, at last.

Tod considered, and shook his head. "Nope, you can't get inside it. Room enough and cool enough now—but there isn't a handhold in there, or on the tube. Can't build them into the lining."

He reached out wildly as Jerry slipped out of the clamps, and floated free on a single rope. Jerry brought up with a weak jerk at the end of the rope and reached down with the long pick he'd been holding. His stomach heaved violently, but he couldn't close his eyes. He caught the edge of the tube and pulled himself down. Then he touched his helmet to the metal, and waited until Tod bent over.

Sound traveled easily through the metal. "You blamed young idiot!" But there was admiration in Tod's tones as well as anger, and Jerry needed that encouragement.

"Let out the rope, Tod," he ordered. "I'll need slack enough to climb back."

He felt the rope slacken carefully. Then, using the pick against one wall of the tube and his feet against the other, he began moving slowly back. It was easier than he expected, as long as he took it slowly. There was no weight to bother him, and the surface of the tube was slightly rough.

At the nozzle, he waited while Tod threw a rope through the hole where the plug had been, and fastened himself down. Now it was comparatively easy to chip off the slag, since his hands could guide the tools easily, and get effective leverage on the hammer. He began smoothing it down, scraping the inside of the nozzle. Luckily, the force of the fuel had cleaned that—or the fuel had dissolved the slag, before it could grow to any size.

Getting out was a simple matter of giving himself a faint push that carried him beyond the tube, and then letting Tod reel him in on the rope around his waist. But after he was drawn down beside the engineer, he stood swaying for long minutes before he could make the trip back into the ship.

If the rope had been too weakened, or if he'd given himself too much speed out of the tube . . .

He let the thought drop, and began following Tod back. The engineer's few words of praise were mixed with descriptions of what a fool he was, but he felt more like a man and a captain.

Inside, he glanced at the clock, and gasped. They had spent eleven hours out there, getting the nozzle cleaned. The jinx that was following the *Last Hope* was working overtime. Now all his carefully prepared course was useless.

CHAPTER 6/

Dead Man's Orbit

JERRY cut on the blast, carefully at first. It felt right—there was no roughness, and the ship answered smoothly, the fuel feed gauge and the pressure indicator going up together as they should. He moved the control up to the full two gees, and sent it a trifle higher.

"Okay, Tod," he decided. "We're on our way again."

The engineer nodded, packed a new wad of Venus gum into his mouth, and slid down the rail, unzipping the space suit with one hand while he held on with the other. Jerry began unfastening his own suit.

The radio buzzed sharply.

He threw a startled glance at it, jerked out of the suit, and moved to the control seat. "Earth ship *Last Hope*. Come in!"

Almost instantly, the answer came back. "Venus ship *Dawn Maid*, Carlson speaking. You're Blaine?"

"Jerry Blaine. Where are you?"

"Just out of your radar range, apparently. Our radar is a little stronger, it seems, and we spotted you. It seemed like a good chance to say hello. We're heading back from Jupiter, but your jets seem to point toward the big fellow. Right?"

Jerry admitted it, with a sinking sensation. The Venus ship had proved fast on the way to the Moon, but hardly that fast. "How'd you do it?"

A laugh came over the phones. "We didn't hit Mars—we went straight on, and we're bound back for Mars now. But from the way you're heading, you shouldn't worry. What are you carrying? Three gees? You must be, if you're going to brake down to Jupiter, judging speed and distance! I thought at first you might be a tail-ender, days behind, but now I guess you must have hit inward to Mercury and our planet first, eh?"

He must have heard Jerry's sudden startled gasp. His soft voice stopped quickly, and a touch of worry crept into it. "You're not in trouble, are you?"

"No trouble," Jerry assured him quickly. "Just realized it's time to change my course. I've got to turn over! Look, I'm going to have to cut off, but you've been a big help."

"Okay, Blaine. We get lonely too. Lots of luck, and may you beat Mars. *Dawn Maid* signing off."

"Luck to you. *Last Hope* off," Jerry acknowledged mechanically.

He tossed the phones back and grabbed for his instruments. Jupiter was too large in the plate now, and the instruments confirmed what he should have known all along. They'd been drifting for eleven hours—enough to bring them over seventy million miles closer to Jupiter. They were well beyond their normal turnover point. The Venusan's comment about the speed he'd need had made him realize it for the first time, but they were already too close to the giant planet for them to decelerate in the time they had at two gees!

He blamed himself for being a fool, though he knew it had been caused by the fatigue of the long hours of hard labor outside. Even without the pull of acceleration, it had left every muscle in his body aching, and numbed the awareness that pilots developed only after years of experience; he'd been a fool, nevertheless. It was his job to consider everything.

His fingers were stiff on the calculator. He didn't try to get completely accurate results, but only to rough in a new course.

With it finished, he reached for the phone and called Tod. "Tod, any chance of stepping up the power from here to Jupiter?"

"A feather, lad." The engineer sounded almost pleased about something, and Jerry felt a bit less ashamed of himself as he realized that the old man hadn't thought of the trouble, either. "Don't they sing pretty now? Every strut in the old ship knows she's back on the beam!"

"Could she take two and a quarter?"

Tod seemed to consider it, and Jerry could almost see the shake of his head as he answered. "Wouldn't try it—she might, but if there's even a trace of that clinker left, she'll foul up when the heat starts building up on us."

Jerry groaned to himself. With the thrust he was feeding in now, the ship would be able to stop eventually—but that would be an hour beyond Jupiter. Then he'd have to swing about and start chasing the moons. And it would bring them into the worst possible position.

He'd already started the reversal, and now he corrected it, until they were pointing back toward the big planet. He eased the control up a trifle, holding it just above two gees. He should have cut off power and reversed at once, he knew—but he'd messed things up again.

All he could do now was to figure his course more carefully. He might have made a mistake—and even a small mistake could make for trouble of worse nature, or leave him worrying about a trouble that wasn't serious after all.

Tod's hand fell on his shoulder. "Best get to bed, Jerry. Nothing you can do now, and it ain't wise to try any figuring while you're all worn out. I'll take over."

Jerry started to protest, but he knew there was sense in the old man's words. He slid out of the seat, and dragged himself to the rail, and down to his hammock.

There was something—something he'd read in a book once. If he could only remember it, it might still get them out of the mess.

He tried to recall it, but his brain was too tired, and sleep hit him almost at once.

Tod had coffee waiting for him when he came back into the control room, hours later. The old man was worn out, too, but he sprang up quickly, trying to cover it up. "Young idiot! Thought I heard you down there. Why didn't you sleep a full ten hours when you could?"

"Because an old idiot up here didn't have sense enough to admit he needed sleep, too," Jerry told him, grinning. It was the right note to strike. The engineer suddenly chuckled gruffly, and went down the rail, muttering something about young fools who woke themselves up, but still grinning.

The smile faded from Jerry's face as he picked up the calculator. The disk of Jupiter was already growing in the tele-plates and through the ports. With a diameter of 86,000 miles, its flattening at the poles and its bands of yellow and red showed up distinctly, even at a distance of many million miles. By straining his eyes, Jerry thought he could just make out the great red spot that had once been considered a boiling sea, but was now known to be only a peculiar atmospheric disturbance.

His finger settled over the calculator as he began figuring their course more carefully. This time he double checked as he went along. The results were only slightly different. They had more speed than they could kill in the time left, and to go past Jupiter would put them into a distribution of the moons around the planet, which would make touching all four inhabited ones a long-drawn-out affair. They'd lose still more precious hours.

The vague idea he'd had before came back to him, and he suddenly realized where he'd seen it. It had been in an old account of early days, in which a not too accurate reporter had described a dip into the atmosphere of Jupiter.

It had probably been pure fiction, but the idea had its merits. With that, they could use the quarter million miles to Jupiter, inside the orbit of Io. Then, by careful steering, they could dip into the upper layers of that vast atmosphere, cutting their speed until it was just enough to break free of Jupiter's pull and carry them up to Io. And by good luck, for a change, Io would be in a good position.

He figured the time carefully, and again began working on the location of the moons. It came out much better that way. They might even make up a few hours that had been lost in the cleaning of the big tube!

He corrected the course to bring them straight to Jupiter, instead of skirting outside along Io's orbit, and fed the proper figures into the automatic pilot.

It wasn't until that was done that he realized it had been more than twenty-four hours since he'd eaten. He went down into the little galley and began rummaging through the supplies near the front. A can of steak caught his eye. He'd been saving it, but this seemed to be as good a time to have it as any other. He pulled it down, together with a can of corn and another of mashed potatoes. Sun Fuels hadn't kicked at the cost of supplies, and Dick had picked out the best, it seemed.

He left half of it in the tray for Tod and carried the heated plastic cans up to the control room. It was too much trouble to bother with plates, and this way saved washing. Tod would have bawled him out, since the engineer was fussy about such things, but Tod was asleep.

He was working on the orbits that led back from Jupiter to Venus or Mercury when he finally heard the old engineer stirring. He heard a snort as the man found the food, and Tod's head appeared in the central shaft.

"Jerry, next time you eat, I want to find a cleaned plate on the rack. This business of eating out of cans is no good—no good at all. Want the *Last Hope* to get cockroaches?"

Jerry grunted a reply, but he knew it wasn't a good time to argue. Tod was always crotchety when he woke up. Anyhow, the boy knew that a ship could get roaches. He'd been on mining ships that were infested, and it hadn't been pleasant. Some of the ships even had rats.

Man usually managed to take his pests along with him. Now Earth had finally gotten rid of most of its vermin, but rats, mice, roaches, and other unpleasant things could be found in the domes of Ganymede and the ships that plied between the worlds.

With his decision made, the hours began to drag. He checked his position regularly, but it seemed to be as it should. He had to be careful with this maneuver, since here even a few miles of error could prove fatal, but there was nothing further for him to do now. Final checkings would have to be made.

He was glad when Tod relieved him again, bringing him his supper on a plate. The old man made no reference to the previous meal, but he managed to create an unusual amount of noise as he set the plate on the control board.

Jerry ate his supper dutifully, making sure he'd picked up all the crumbs, and carried the plate back to the galley. Tod's voice drifted down the shaft. "Make sure that plate is clean, youngster!"

"Who's captain here, anyhow?" Jerry yelled back. But he had already learned that the galley was one place where he wasn't boss, and never would be. Remembering back to other ships he had visited, he realized it wasn't unusual.

He was worried a little about the stunt he planned, but he forced his mind off it. The other sleep hadn't been long enough, he knew, and his eyes seemed to close by themselves.

Tod got him up eight hours later. "Figured we'd have to cut down a bit, lad. I'll take eight myself, and that oughta give us a couple hours to work together on the landing. Right?"

"Fine," Jerry agreed.

Jupiter was a great ball now, he saw. From the control room, it seemed like something hot and molten, as the early astronomers had thought it was. But exploration near it had proved what had been decided early in the twentieth century. It was as cold as the frozen worlds around it had been, with the color coming from the sunlight reflected from its roiling gases.

This time his checkup of his position took longer, and he made a few tiny alterations in the course. He didn't want to go down into that tremendous atmospheric sea, but only to skirt the outermost edge, where his speed would be slowed, but where the friction wouldn't burn up the ship, nor the pressure crush it.

Tod awakened by himself at the end of eight hours. He fussed about quickly and came up with coffee. Then he gasped.

Jupiter was less than two hours away now, and it seemed to fill half the sky. They were heading straight toward its edge.

"Sheer off, lad!" he said sharply. "Don't play with the big fellow."

Jerry shook his head. "Can't help it, Tod. We can't kill enough speed otherwise. I'm going into a braking orbit to save time."

The older man put the coffee down slowly, staring at Jerry. "Are you serious? You're crazy! Now I know all Blaines are loco. Do you know what a braking orbit is? You hit the air, just kissing it. You slow down, but you go on out. Then the planet pulls you back, and you hit the air again. Each time you go around and dip back, you get closer. You're swinging like a kid on a rope around a pole. You don't just touch it and go off."

"You do if you need to lose part of your speed. Anyhow, I remember other men doing it. Going from Ganymede to Io, wasn't it?"

Tod shook his head. "It's been tried, lad. Jupiter has a mighty pretty ship somewhere down there, with three of the best pilots and a crew—because Jim Thorpe tried it back in the early days when he was drunk. We got his radio messages for a while. And a lot of these fool writers claim it has been done. Maybe so—I never heard of the guy who did it."

"But—"

"But nothing. That's why they call it Dead Man's Orbit, after poor old Jim. And he was drunk at the time, or he wouldn't have tried it. Sheer off!"

Jerry looked down at the planet, frowning. The fear in Tod's voice was genuine. And now that he thought of it, he didn't remember it mentioned as having been done in the books on navigation, though they'd covered the theory of it. He felt his face tighten as horror began to creep through him.

"I can't sheer off, Tod. We're too close. We're only about an hour away, and I've already turned over to hit it head on, in case I have to feed extra thrust to break free!"

Tod stood there, staring at the planet for a few seconds more, while he slowly stuffed Venus gum into his mouth and began chewing. His shoulders seemed to sag under what he saw, and he shook his head. Jerry watched him, and the ball of fear in his stomach grew larger and threatened to explode.

"I guess I made a complete idiot of myself this time, Tod," he said miserably.

The old man shook himself, and turned back.

"Maybe. Maybe not. Jim Thorpe never had fuel like ours, either—and he didn't have a ship that was built to work the asteroids, even if they did weaken her. And maybe I'm getting old, like Dick says, and fussy. Just an old hen clucking over her chicks. Don't let me bother you, boy!"

He picked up the orbit Jerry had drawn and dropped into the seat beside the boy, studying it. Tod had never learned navigation, but he'd had to do a lot of piloting around the asteroid belt, and he could read an orbit.

He nodded at last.

"Well?" Jerry asked, as the engineer continued to stare at the orbit.

"Maybe. But you'll have to hit it just right. You're still going too fast. The *Last Hope* is a sweet ship, boy, but she can melt down, if the friction's too much. If she goes up to a few hundred degrees, she can take it. She can't take a thousand. And the vanes for steering—well, we tested 'em out at seven gees, and they hardly bent. But all the same, they can be ripped smack off."

"But you think we can make it?" Jerry insisted.

"Nope. If we do, I'll cook every meal and wash every dish from here back to Earth. I think we're done for. But I ain't sure. I'm going to get myself down there in the engine room and I'm going to start praying like I never prayed in my life. Only don't you do it—you stick to your piloting!"

He patted Jerry on the back, and reached for the rail. Jerry watched him, looking for some sign. The engineer halted, and shrugged. "I guess I don't feel like I'm set for dying yet, at that," he said, and began sliding down.

It was doubtful comfort to Jerry. He wiped the sweat off his hands.

Jupiter was growing larger by the minute now, and its atmosphere suddenly looked like a sea of death and poison. He stared at it, half-hypnotized by its menace. Then he jerked his eyes away. When he looked back, it seemed normal again.

Armstrong had been a crazy fool to try to land on the Moon, and the first man on Mars had expected to die there before they could send a second ship—but they'd both lived. Jerry didn't feel ready to die yet, either.

CHAPTER 7 /

Jupiter Calling

MINUTE by minute, they were drawing down into the frightful maw of the planet. The atmosphere no longer looked like a solid crust, but began to show disturbances and evidences of local winds. Clouds of methane and ammonia bigger than all of Earth whipped by in its hydrogen layers.

It seemed to be wracked by storms of every kind. Even without them, it would have been frightening. For all its huge size, it rotated on its axis once every ten hours, so rapidly that it had flattened at the poles and bulged out at the equator.

As they drew nearer, the familiar trick of vision turned it from a ball under them to a big bowl over them. It seemed to be opening a mouth and calling to them, hungrily.

Jerry had made the last possible correction before they touched the atmosphere. Now he sat, his hands on the steering-vane controls, and his feet poised delicately over the pedals that controlled the steering rockets and the thrust of the big tube; the hand controls were more familiar, but he couldn't use them while controlling the vanes.

The faintest whisper of a sound reached him, like a high shriek, and for a moment he thought that the planet was actually calling. Then he knew they had touched the first thin wisps of atmosphere.

He moved the controls and felt a faint resistance from the ship. They were plunging deeper now, and he began to try to flatten out.

His eyes stuck to the hull pyrometers that would show when the skin of the ship was too hot—he hoped. There still wasn't enough air out there to be measured by anything but the most delicate instrument. But at high enough a speed, that was still too thick; the faster he was going, the more molecules of the gas he would hit per second—and the more heat woud be created from the friction.

Time seemed to slow to nothing. He was still sinking, and the whistle became a full shriek in his ears. He forced the vanes back a bit more, and felt the controlling motors groan as they took the strain. Now they seemed to be in a level position, skimming through the atmosphere without moving up or down—but he knew they were still sinking. The heat on the skin was going up.

He began to try to pull out. The coldness of the atmosphere—cold enough to liquefy Earth's air— helped somewhat to keep the ship's temperature down, but it wasn't enough.

He didn't dare use the vanes any harder. The steering rockets went on as his foot hit them, and the ship swung faintly.

Jupiter was pulling now, trying to suck him down. The call of the planet was stronger. At the surface, its gravity was nearly three times that of Earth—greater than the maximum thrust of the rocket, for more than a few minutes. If he lost too much speed, he'd be pulled down hopelessly. If he lost too little, the whole maneuver would be wasted.

But he was no longer worried about that. He wanted to get out!

He held the vanes back as far as he dared—barely out of position. He kicked the big tube on to full blast. And bit by bit, they seemed to be coming out of it.

Even through the insulated walls of the ship, heat was pouring in. The skin must be getting dangerously close to the overheated stage, but he didn't have time to look. His strain indicators were more important now.

"Hull's hot, but still standing," Tod's whisper sounded beside him. He hadn't seen the engineer crawl into the control room, and he didn't look now. But the presence of the other gave him some measure of confidence again.

The shriek was lower now. They were beginning to come out of the atmosphere. But it was still a struggle to keep the ship lifting.

Then it was only a whisper. And suddenly, it was gone, and the vane motors cut off before they could overrun. There was no atmosphere outside, and they were heading out into space again.

Now the pull of Jupiter would help to slow them.

Jerry gulped once, and began checking position furiously. He was amazed to find that they had come out almost exactly where his orbit had indicated. By sheer luck, without any thanks to his ability to follow that crazy orbit, they had swung around and emerged just where he'd wanted.

His hands were stiff from strain, but he threw on the steering rockets and began a savage reversal to bring the big tube out where it could slow them toward Io. And again luck played on his side, letting him correct his swing with a single, even blast from the side rockets.

Then he dropped his hands to his side, sighed once, and fainted!

It was only a few seconds later when he came to, and he was grateful that Tod apparently hadn't noticed his blackout. The old man sat with his eyes on the tele-panels. His mouth was slightly open. Then he closed it, shook himself, and turned slowly to Jerry.

"Good to see the stars," he said, as he lifted himself from the seat. "Well, I guess I'm gonna be doing the cooking and dishes for the rest of this blamed trip. Thought sure you'd save me the trouble, though."

Jerry tried to answer, but the words were stuck somewhere down in his stomach. The old man chuckled and reached out a leathery hand. He shook Jerry's trembling fingers once, firmly, and then dropped back down toward the engines.

Jerry tried to get up, but something held him back. He looked down curiously. He had no memory of ever buckling on the straps that were designed to protect a pilot from sudden violent acceleration or deceleration, but they were laced up firmly. He must have done it out of habit, just before entering the atmosphere of Jupiter, and it had probably saved his life.

Probably Tod had been buckled in, too. Or perhaps he had doubled himself into the ball that the school taught for emergencies, so that his body braced itself from every direction. How'd he ever reached the control room, Jerry couldn't guess. But Tod had grown up when they were still using high-acceleration ships, and he'd have known how to care for himself.

Jerry wasn't worried about the answers to his questions as he unfastened himself. He was too busy enjoying the feeling of being alive, and of knowing that somehow he'd brought them both through.

His fingers were still shaky as he reached for his navigating instruments and began locating Io and plotting his course. It was similar to the one he had already drawn, and that helped.

They were halfway to the moon when the alarm suddenly sounded. Jerry's eyes jerked to the tele-panel, and then to the radar screen. Something was coming toward the ship at an orbit which threatened collision. He threw in higher magnification and saw that it was a large body, probably a hundred miles in diameter.

Jupiter's closest moon! It lacked a name, and was simply known as V, since it was the fifth to be discovered. He checked the screen again, and jerked out the chart of the moons. A quick estimate showed him that they would come close to it, but that there would be no collision, and he punched the *overlook* button on the radar. The alarms went off, though the pip that indicated the planetoid stayed on the screen.

For a moment, he wondered whether it would alter the course by its gravity pull, but a little checking reassured him. He'd pass it by a distance of fifty miles or so, and it was too small and weak to bother him in his course toward Io.

He'd forgotten about it, since the original course didn't include so near an approach to Jupiter. Moons VI, VII, and X seven millions miles out, and the three at fourteen million miles—VIII, IX and XI—were all tiny things, but he'd checked their position when passing near their orbits. None had proved of any importance, though the fact that the outer three rotated around Jupiter in the opposite direction from the others was still a matter of curiosity to him and to the astronomers.

He watched the little fifth moon slide by, too far for any sharp details to show. It was sometimes used as an observation post for scientists studying Jupiter, and he'd seen pictures of it. But he could see only a small ball, with none of the rocky roughness he had expected.

Io was now visible in his tele-panel. It was about the size of Earth's moon, and he was less than half the distance from Earth to Luna Center, which made some of the surface markings plain to his eyes. Originally, Io had been only a place for mines, but the mines had proved richer than suspected at first, and a true colony had gradually grown up there.

Jerry watched Io come toward him, while the rocket

tube went on cutting his speed. He was braking faster than he needed, and he reduced the thrust a trifle, until he was sure that the zero speed would be reached just as he touched the little planet.

There was a crowd in space suits out on the field as he came down, and he frowned. They couldn't know of his plunge into Jupiter? He didn't want any talk of it now—he was still ashamed of the ignorance and vanity that had led him to tackle it. And reports going back to the other planets might make him something of a hero—but they'd also make him the laughingstock of anyone who guessed the whole story.

He set down a bit bumpily, and glanced at the clock. It was ten-thirty in the forenoon, Sunday. The trip from Mars to Io had taken ninety-nine and a half hours, and he was now only ninety-two and a half behind schedule, in spite of the tube cleaning.

He came out to find a crowd of spacemen waiting, all of them bearing the insignia of rocket freighters. One of them came over and touched helmets with Jerry, since there was no air here to carry sound.

"Dead Man's Orbit? We figured it had to be when we caught your flare in the telescope. Couldn't come from that direction any other way. Congratulations, kid—always wondered when some of these guys would realize modern ships ain't like the old ones. How was it?"

There was none of the amusement he'd expected when he saw who they were. He shook his head, making scratching sounds against the other's helmet. "Rugged. My engineer and I thought we were dead. If I hadn't been such a fool—"

The other laughed lazily, and there was amusement in his voice now. "Sure. Takes a fool to do it the first time or so." Then his voice sobered. "But you got out alive—and in this business, that's what counts."

They'd retreated to a little building beside the field, and moved in through the air lock. The other men threw off their helmets, inside, and began clustering around Jerry and Todd, shaking their hands.

Tod grinned at his confusion. "Every rocket man who ever lived was a crazy fool, lad," he said. "Ain't it so, boys?"

The chorus of agreeing yells was unanimous. Then the leader sobered.

"We came out to give you a hand. Figured you'd need a good going over after all that. You never know what strains get set up in a ship. It'll take a few hours— not much, though—but it'll be a blamed sight safer. And we'll load you up while we're at it."

He brushed off Jerry's thanks and began giving directions. Men began streaming out toward the *Last Hope*. One of them motioned Jerry and Tod out toward a waiting tractor, and they followed him. To Jerry's surprise, the inside of the little machine was airtight, and they could remove their helmets.

The driver headed the machine toward the domed city that stood a mile away. "This is a spaceman's world, kid; we do half the shipping for the moons. That and mining is what keeps us going. And when anybody comes here with a new trick up his sleeve about handling a ship, he's *in*. Of course, on the other moons, you'll find a bunch of farmers. They'll expect you to get up and give speeches. You like speeches?"

Jerry grunted in disgust, and the man laughed.

"Yeah, we figured as much. We'll hold back the word on you till you're bound back for the inner planets, then. What do you think of our moon?"

Jerry didn't think too much of it, either good or bad. It was at least two hundred degrees below zero, without a breath of air, and as harsh as the asteroids he had known as a boy. But he liked what he'd seen of the people, just as he'd always liked the rough-and-ready miners.

He stared at the tiny dome that represented a quarter of the population of Io. It was a smaller version of the one at Luna Center, except that here the entire outer wall was filled with growing things which must provide them with their food. Luna Center depended on Earth for most of its goods, but the Ionians must grow all their own.

He signed in at the local office of the Commission, and tried to check up on his progress, as compared to the other racers. It was impossible to be sure from the scattered reports that had come over the tight-beam interplanet radio. At a wild guess, Mars was well ahead of him, and only Ganymede was behind. It didn't look good.

At the Commissioner's insistence, he let them serve him a meal at the local restaurant, and was surprised to find that the food was as good as any he had tasted. But in spite of his guide's assurances that he'd be notified in plenty of time, he was unable to concentrate on the food. He wanted to get back to the ship.

Tod had already gone back, to supervise the final checkup.

Finally, he climbed back into the little tractor, and they began the return journey, this time by another route that took them past one of the mines. It was covered with a little dome of its own, and a few men were busy loading ore into one of the tractors, but there was nothing else to see.

The ship was a beehive of activity, and there was nothing he could do. He'd only get in the way of these men. They knew ships, and they were being thorough about things.

It was three-thirty P.M. when it was finished, and they pronounced the *Last Hope* fit as a fiddle. The men weren't waiting for his thanks, but were already getting into their tractors and heading back toward the dome. He waved at them, and they waved back. Then the *Last Hope* lifted for Europa.

Tod was familiar with the second colony out from

Jupiter, but it was all new to Jerry. He found the people there more like Earth than anywhere else. The planet was covered with what looked like ice, but was actually frozen air and water in separate layers. Instead of domes, they had dug deep into the surface, and their chief resource seemed to be the atmosphere. They heated it to provide oxygen for their living quarters, and mined it in great slabs for shipment to the other moons.

In their underground gardens, in tanks of water and chemicals which they imported from Io, they grew what looked like enough food to feed a dozen worlds. Much of it went to Callisto and Ganymede, though some of it was shipped back as far as the asteroids.

There was no trouble there. The Commission representative met them at their little field, signed their papers, and wished them good speed, while their tanks were refilled with their special fuel. It took only a few minutes, since little fuel had been used.

They reached Callisto at three A.M., Monday. Like Io, it was a mining world, and airless. The dome was larger, though, and there were more people. Jerry got a few glimpses of the domes beyond as he rode in to see the Commission agent. Most of the colony here was clustered within fifty miles of the major mine, where great supplies of uranium came forth to furnish the whole Solar System.

With a diameter of only 3,200 miles, the little planet should have had very little of the heavy elements, but this freak deposit seemed to be bottomless. They had been mining it for a hundred years, and it looked as rich as ever.

Jerry was getting sick of the moons with their short jumps, where there was no chance to make up time. He heaved a sign of relief as they took off. "Next stop Ganymede, and then back toward the sun!" he announced.

Tod nodded glumly. "Next stop trouble. Ganymede won't like us. After Earth got done dumping prisoners there, Mars started taking over."

Jerry could see nothing that could be done there, but he worried about it. They'd gone too long without bad luck, and it was time the jinx hit them again.

CHAPTER 8 /

Delay on Ganymede

GANYMEDE lay between the orbits of Europa and Callisto, and was about the same size as the latter moon. As Tod MacLane had said, it had once been used as a prison colony by Venus, Earth and Mars, before the moons were colonized generally. Most of the prisoners, though, had come from the heavily populated Earth. Even though there was no longer any such practice, it was only natural that a good deal of resentment should exist there for the mother world of the human race.

Mars had probably made full use of that. There were rumors that the governor of Ganymede was actually chosen on Mars, and that the last election had been only a joke. But there was no proof of that.

It was another airless world, but a thriving one. Strange plants that could grow without air and in the bitter cold had been found there. They were totally unlike any normal form of vegetation found on Earth or Mars, and seemed to depend on the radioactivity of the minerals around for their growth. But odd as they were, they were still protoplasm. They had yielded a whole host of new drugs, as well as a good deal of information on the whole nature of life.

That and large deposits of pure beryllium had made

the little moon fairly rich. It boasted an enclosed landing field, like the Moon, and the domed city behind the field was the largest one in the Solar System. It held almost fifty thousand people, and there were other domes almost as big.

Jerry landed cautiously, and surveyed the group on the field with considerable misgiving. They seemed to be cheering him, but he doubted the sincerity of their cheers.

Tod was openly suspicious. Like most spacemen, he believed that all the people on Ganymede were crooks, and that they made a practice of stealing the claims on all the good asteroids. Since they were the nearest fully-authorized claim office, it would have been easy enough for them.

Jerry had no use for such beliefs. The children of criminals usually turned out to be normal people, he knew. His doubts were nothing but superstition, and he knew it, but he couldn't quiet them. There'd been trouble on the Moon and trouble on Mars. It seemed unbelievable that there should be nothing but good luck around Jupiter.

He didn't like the looks on the faces. They were filled with the same enmity he had found on Mars, but this was snarling and nasty, rather than gruff and rude. That might have had something to do with the attitude of spacemen, of course. But Jerry found himself heartily disliking the narrow-eyed suspicion in their glances.

Yet everything seemed to be as it should. He found his fuel waiting for him, and there were men enough about to load it along with the supplies he'd need for the long hop to the inner planets. They moved forward briskly, and began work without a wasted motion.

A tractor-taxi was standing near, but the driver shook his head, motioning toward the gate leading out onto the surface, then jerking a thumb backward. Jerry looked around and found a gaudily painted trimobile like those used on Earth. The driver opened the door.

"Tractors go outside. We use this in the city," he explained. "The Commission office, I suppose?"

Jerry climbed in with a nod, wondering. On the outer planets, most of the workers were descended from poor people who had been shipped out to open up the planets, and the men who had first come to Ganymede against their wishes had been even poorer. But the driver's tones, like those of the others he had seen, had all been those of educated men. Either the planet was filled with college graduates, or else the men serving him were a long way from the simple laborers and drivers they seemed.

But still everything seemed to go well. The Commission agent barely glanced at his papers before putting the official scroll on it.

"You're fortunate," he said. "The radio hasn't been working for days—terrific solar static. We just got official word that you were an acceptable replacement for your brother. Incidentally, Mars sends word he's recovering nicely."

Jerry went out feeling more kindly toward Ganymede. Even the occasional grim-faced Martian on the street didn't disturb him.

He found Tod scowling and scratching his head. The work was going along at a rapid rate, and there had obviously been no trouble. Apparently, that was what had been bothering the engineer. He'd expected delays, and he couldn't understand why there were none.

The field official came up, smiling. "The work will be done in ten minutes, Captain Blaine. We've instructions to open the dome whenever you're ready."

"Thanks. I appreciate—"

The howl of a sirene cut off Jerry's words. Tod's beady eyes snapped wider open, and the engineer straightened, with a look that told Jerry he'd been expecting something.

The boy jerked his eyes toward the trimobile that came screaming into the landing dome. It flipped about sharply, turning on one front wheel, and headed toward him, the siren still disturbing the air.

A big man in ornate official uniform jumped out of it in front of Jerry. "Who's the pilot of that ship?"

"I am," Jerry admitted.

"How old are you?"

Jerry reached for his certificate from the Commission, and held it out. "Seventeen. But I've passed all the tests, and this gives me authority."

The man handed it back without glancing at it. He motioned to someone in the trimobile, and another uniformed figure came out. This one headed for the ship, and began climbing the ladder. Tod let out a cry, and Jerry started forward.

The big official held him back. "We're sealing the ship. According to the law here, no pilot can use this field, or land or remove a ship, unless he's of legal age."

"But this isn't local. This is Commission business—and they work under an interplanetary agreement. Ganymede belongs to the racing union!"

"I've got my orders." The official watched the other come back from the ship, and jerked a hand toward Tod. "Keep this man on the field, and away from the ship. You, young man, will come with me. If there's any clause permitting you to leave, Judge Condon can take care of such matters."

This time the trimobile seemed in no hurry, and the siren wasn't in use. Jerry tried to argue with the official on the way back, but the man wouldn't talk, and even refused to listen. The driver grinned back once, nastily.

They finally reached the courthouse, but there was a long line of men waiting to be tried ahead of Jerry, and no amount of argument would persuade them to put him ahead of the others. He noticed that the supposed prisoners were laughing and joking among themselves. As Jerry watched, one was being sentenced to six months in jail for stealing a trimobile. The man looked anything but worried about it, and he winked as a policeman led him away.

It wasn't hard to guess that the court had been deliberately filled with men who would be tried for offenses they had never committed and sentenced to terms they would have to fill. It was a clever way to keep him waiting, and there was nothing he could do about it. With Tod confined to the field, he couldn't hope that the engineer could get to the Commission agent, either.

But it didn't make sense; they'd probably just passed the law when they found he was coming and learned his age. There were plenty of pilots who were under twenty-one.

They couldn't make it stick before the Commission—but they probably didn't mean to. Even if their own ship was ruled out of the race, they had nothing to lose, since it had no chance to win, according to the reports he had received before. They'd be content to see him kept from any chance of victory, and to make sure that Mars could win.

He stood up suddenly, shouting to the judge. "I demand to be removed from this court! As a citizen of Earth, operating under Earth laws, this court has no right to try me."

The judge rapped his gavel smartly to quiet Jerry, and then dropped it.

"Why not, young man?" Condon wanted to know.

"Because you operate on the Martian code, and by the charter that granted freedom to the planets, a case of mixed law can be tried only by an interplanet court, without the defendant's consent!"

He felt safe in that, as there was no interplanet court on Ganymede. However, the fuss would be enough to bring his case to the attention of the Commission representative, if he was lucky.

Condon considered it, apparently wondering whether he could get away with a violation of such a charter ruling. It was an escape clause seldom invoked, since the interplanet courts sometimes took years to decide, but Jerry was within his rights.

"Very well, then," Condon decided. "Will you consent to be tried here?"

"On two conditions—that I receive immediate trial, and that I be granted all the privileges of a citizen of the Martian code while being tried!"

Condon nodded slowly. The prisoners stopped laughing and began to get up and file out. The police made no effort to stop them. The game was over, and the court no longer cared about keeping up a pretense.

Condon pulled out a thick book which contained the major laws of the Martian code. It was an honest code, too, Jerry knew. As a navigator-trainee, he'd had to study some of it, since his work would bring him to Mars or Ganymede where it was in force. In many ways, it was both simpler and fairer than the older Earth code.

Jerry accepted it, knowing that his taking the book meant that he was willing to dispense with legal advice, and depend on it for his case. The judge propped another copy up on the bench before him.

"According to Ganymedan law," he began, "no pilot may enter or depart from a Ganymedan port unless he shall be of legal age and his ship shall be suitably registered to his authority. You have entered the port with your ship, the *Last Hope*. You admit that?"

"I do. It's suitably registered to my authority," Jerry answered.

"Quite so. But you also admit that you are not of legal age?"

"As I told the officer, I'm seventeen. I admit that."

"Good. What defense have you?"

Jerry shrugged faintly. "I knew of no such law, your honor. I came here without being warned of it, under authority of the Armstrong Classic Commission. By general agreement, local laws do not affect officers, crews, or ships in the Classic."

The judge frowned.

"Your claim of ignorance may be true, and this court will accept it, since no claim has been made to the contrary. You are therefore absolved from any sentence for entering. But that does not apply to your leaving, since you do know the law now. As for the freedom granted racing pilots, that is only a courtesy. Obviously, entering the race cannot give them the power to rob or to kill on any local port. In this case, I find that the law requires me to deny you the right to remove your ship without the arrival of a properly authorized pilot of legal age."

"But I am of legal age," Jerry stated flatly.

"You admitted you were not!"

Jerry shook his head. "I did not. I admitted that I was seventeen. But under the Martian code—page 1243, section II, according to the index—legal age is defined as sixteen years, based on the interplanet calendar. And the interplanet calendar uses an Earth year as its base."

"But—"

The judge stopped, and thought it over. He'd agreed to grant Jerry all the privileges of a citizen under the Martian code for the purposes of the trial, which meant that he couldn't retreat now to the Earth code legal age of twenty-one.

He grinned wryly, and Jerry knew that his guess as to the judge's thoughts had been correct. "Very well. The court finds the defendant was wrongly deprived of his rights."

He motioned Jerry out, and the boy lost no time in going. Then he swung back quietly, realizing that he had received no order for the removal of the seals on the ship.

But the judge had anticipated him. "The court is recessed until tomorrow!" he declared, and moved back to his chambers, leaving Jerry to face an empty bench.

Jerry found a cab outside, and directed the driver to

the Commission agency. It moved off at a snail's pace, managing to miss almost every traffic light. It took an hour to reach the agency. Then the representative was having lunch, and no one knew where he had gone!

Jerry cooled his heels, fuming. He'd felt pleased with himself for remembering the age of majority under the Martian code and using it so neatly. Then he'd had to go and ruin it all by carelessness in not demanding immediately that the ship be unsealed. Without a court order, the field authorities would never let him aboard.

Tod must be going crazy while he had to wait for the agent to return. He was sure that the man was honest— Commission agents might have their prejudices, but they were careful to be fair in the actions and their decisions. They had never been any charge leveled against the two men who ran the Classic.

He was apparently right. When the agent came back and heard of the situation, he went into action. But more delays were inevitable. No one knew where the judge was, and no one had any idea where he could be reached. The agent called the governor, but he was also away.

"And I can't prove that he isn't," he growled to Jerry. "We know it's a stall, but there's no proof. Come on, we'll make a tour. We may be able to locate someone."

Even the minor officials seemed to be away for the day, or sick. Disgusted, the agent of the Commission finally gave up, and thought it over. Then he headed the trimobile back to the rocket port.

Jerry watched in surprise as he moved forward and began wrapping a small chain around the lock to the field dome. A field official came running over.

"I'm closing this port, pending an investigation of the case against Jerry Blaine," the agent announced loudly. "This requires full evidence, and until the Commission can send a committee to examine the facts, I have to be sure no evidence is removed from the field."

Tod was signaling from inside the field dome, and Jerry waved back. But his mind was busy wondering whether the bluff would work—if it was a bluff. The powers of the Commission were extensive, and the agent might be within his rights.

In less than ten minutes, Judge Condon drove up in a car driven by a policeman, huffing and puffing as he ran toward the Commission representative.

"It's all a misunderstanding!" the judge was crying. "Just a case of misunderstanding. The governor tells me you think we're trying this young man. I let him free hours ago!"

"And my ship?" Jerry asked.

The judge tried to look surprised, but he was too exhausted to put on a good act. "Of course, of course. Here, I've brought an order with me! You know there's no case to be investigated, young man!"

Jerry nodded as the field workers ran toward the ship to remove the seal. He wished he could rail at them the way Tod was doing, but he was unable to think of anything beyond his need to get the ship up and on her way.

It was only a few minutes later that the all-clear signal dropped, and he blasted off. The clock showed that it was ten P.M., Monday the sixteenth—and they'd lost sixteen hours on Ganymede. Now, a hundred and four hours off Dick's schedule, they were farther behind in the race than ever.

And less than half of the race was completed.

CHAPTER 9/

Mars Strikes Again

BEFORE, coming toward Jupiter, Jerry had been running at an angle which put him slightly out of the paths of the rocks and debris that floated around Jupiter, like tiny moonlets. But on the outward trip, the rules of the race called for him to stick to the plane of the ecliptic and to pass through the asteroid belt. The chances of his hitting one of the orbital chunks of stone were small, but he wasn't counting on luck any more. He forced back the fatigue and stuck to his piloting.

He was still disgusted with himself for wasting so much time on Ganymede. He'd been warned to watch them and should have asked the Commission agent to go back to the ship with him in the first place. Then he'd been careless about the ship after his half-victory over Judge Condon.

He could blame the trouble on the Moon and Mars to the trickery of the red planet. But the rest of his troubles were his own fault, and not bad luck. The dip into Jupiter's atmosphere had been sheer foolishness, caused by half-thinking. It had gained a little time, but it had been lost again by more half-thinking on Ganymede.

It was time he grew up, he decided, if he was to call

himself a pilot. It was his duty to get the ship back to Earth, and to do that, he'd have to examine things thoroughly, and make sure his decisions were more than snap judgments. He'd been running this like a kid's race, instead of serious business.

Mars was smarter there; she might not play fair, but she played carefully. Not one of the tricks could be proved against her. And she wasn't risking lives, he realized suddenly. When it came to a man's ability to go on living, Mars was as decent as the next planet.

Or maybe that was smart too. Except for the clogged rocket nozzle—which might have been an honest bit of bad luck—nothing she had done endangered anyone aboard the *Last Hope*. Mars didn't want Earth to wash out; it was much better for her to have Earth come in last, or to give up after only part of the race had been won. That would be much more disgraceful than blowing up.

It also meant that Jerry couldn't count on the fact that Mars was still bucking him to indicate he was a serious menace to her chances of winning; they wanted him to make the worst possible showing, and would go on fighting him, even if he was already in last place.

Tod brought up food. The engineer had insisted on going on with his offer to do all the cooking and cleaning; Jerry suspected that he actually wanted it that way.

"How's she look down there?" he asked the older man.

Tod shifted his Venus gum and frowned, his bushy eyebrows meeting over his nose. "*Looks* all right. But I don't like it. I'll bet they did something to us, more'n just holding us up! I've been checking up. Going back to it now."

Jerry nodded, feeling an uneasy suspicion that the old man was right. The ship was running smoothly now, with almost no sound from the tube, since the Io spacemen had overhauled her. He heard Tod go back and begin his inspection again. The engineer was whistling uneasily, which indicated he was seriously worried.

There was good reason to worry. They would be safe for a while, once they were beyond Jupiter's moons, but they had to be in first-class condition when they reached the asteroids. Those little broken fragments of a world that had once circled the sun between Mars and Jupiter were rough passage. They came in all sizes, from bits of sand to worlds the size of Ceres, 480 miles in diameter.

Their hundreds of orbits crossed and crisscrossed wildly, and no pilot could plot them all. Jerry knew them better than most men in the race would, but he'd still need perfect response from his rockets to get them through. More racers had died in passing through them than in all the rest of the course.

He went down to the engine room finally, but there was nothing he could do but watch Tod's nervous pacing from indicator to indicator. Jerry followed him about, but the controlling valves and indicators all seemed to be behaving properly.

The big tube was balanced so completely that hardly a sound came through the insulation. Jerry put his ear against the main fuel line and listened. "Gurgling like a baby," he said. "I guess you were wrong, Tod."

"Yeah. Gurgling—*gurgling?*" The little engineer made a single leap that carried him across the room, in spite of the thrust that doubled their weight. "You're right—I knew something was bothering my ears! Shouldn't make a sound."

He listened for half a second more and began reaching for the main valve, screwing it in rapidly with the manual control. The thrust fell off, and suddenly stopped, leaving them weightless.

"Something in the fuel?" Jerry guessed, and the engineer nodded.

Jerry lent a quick hand, while the old man began unscrewing a plug in the line beside a little valve. Black fuel began to run out into the plastic bag Tod held below it. Here, without weight, any liquid tended to break into little round drops and go drifting about messily, unless held in a container.

It ran clear for a few seconds, and then something lumpy oozed through slowly. Tod let it fall into the container, and then screwed back the plug, catching the few tiny drops floating about on a piece of waste that soaked them up. He was careful not to touch the fuel with his hands as he fished the heavier substance out of the plastic container.

He spread it on a sheet of metal, pushing at it with a little wrench handle. "Tar! Half dissolved in the fuel. Jerry, if a good-sized lump of that came through, it'd clog the nozzle for sure—do the same to the steering jets. We've gotta filter the whole shebang!"

"How long?" Jerry asked.

"Won't know till I see how many tanks got this stuff in them. Wait a minute."

Jerry tried to guess how much margin of time they would have. They were four hours out from Ganymede, and well past the dangerous section. But Jupiter's pull was strong, even at this distance, and they'd be losing speed steadily, if slowly. He'd figured that their course would bring them through the next layer of rocks that circled the big planet while the space was fairly clear, according to the information he'd gotten from the spacemen on Io. Most of the rocks beyond Callisto's orbit were bunched in two positions. But without power, they would coast up too slowly, and might crash squarely into the first grouping of the debris.

Tod's yell of misery interrupted his thoughts, and he floated up the shaft to the narrow passageways between the tanks of fuel. The engineer was crouched over one of them, hanging in mid-air and fishing delicately with a long rod through a small hole. His face looked as if his only friend had kicked him in the stomach.

"Every one of 'em! The stinkers got their gunk into the whole shebang! Six tanks, all filled with tar lumps!" He used the rod as a prod, and shoved himself back down beside Jerry. "Kid, we'll be stuck here half a day on this stuff. I should have tested it before I let those lousy crooks touch the fuel taps."

"We've got no more than five hours for the job," Jerry told him. He began explaining about the danger from the bits of rock that lay waiting for them.

Tod groaned. "If I had an empty, I could pump it from a full tank into that through a bucket of waste. The tank flush pumps would do it. Then we could run on one tank while we took care of the others. But they're all full to the gills—and we're gonna need the whole kaboodle if we're gonna reach Venus at full steam. This way, though, we're gonna have to cut pipe and fix up a filter in the feed lines. And we don't have the tools to do that right."

"Isn't there any way to put a filter over the drain in the tank. Sort of a wire cage around it, to hold the filter in place?"

Tod shook his head. His body flipped back and forth under it; any motion in space when their gravity was zero automatically balanced by some opposite movement.

"Build one out of sheet metal, with holes punched in it. Line it with waste, stick another metal can inside that, and screw it down to the drain." He shrugged his shoulders, lifting his feet off the floor for a moment. "Only we don't have anything that'll reach down to the bottom and screw it down, even if I welded it together."

Jerry pressed his toes down lightly, and floated up to the top of the room, where he hitched himself over one of the tanks. He could see that there was a large manhole there, and a smaller, transparent plastic section for viewing the inside of the tank. It seemed to be completely full, until he realized that the liquid would have spread over all the walls of the tanks, without the rocket thrust to hold it down.

"How full are they, anyhow?" he called down.

"A few gallons missing. Maybe thirty gallons in all of them."

They could pump the fuel out of one and into the others until five were completely filled and the sixth would have the smallest possible amount left. He shouted down orders for Tod to set the pumps going. With thirty gallons missing from the one tank, it might work.

"Better start building your filter, Tod," he suggested as he forced himself back down again, catching a handhold to prevent bouncing back. "I'll screw it down. And Tod, make sure there's no tin in it!"

The engineer seemed puzzled, but he turned toward the engine room. "Don't worry. I saw what happened to your dad's ship, lad. No tin!"

Jerry checked his position carefully. The five-hour estimate he'd given the engineer was close enough. If they could get the tube going in that length of time, they should be safe. If they didn't—well, they might still be lucky and avoid a collision with one of the miniature satellites, but they might not! The chances seemed about even.

He pulled the space suit out of its closet and began buckling it on, pulling the straps as tight as he could get them. He didn't want any excess bulges of air this time to lighten him. Even so, he'd need heavy weights to hold him down in the thick, heavy liquid. He replaced the heavy space mittens with the lightest gloves that came with the suit. They were still clumsy, but they were the best he could do.

He checked his air tank carefully, and then headed down the shaft toward the engine room, taking it in a single long glide. The glare of the little electric welder was already lighting the room as he checked his landing and turned around. Tod was welding a threaded nipple to a section of metal plate. He'd already cut most of the parts.

The engineer glanced up as Jerry came over, and a look of sudden comprehension crossed his face. His voice was muffled by the thick helmet. "There are times I figure you've got brains, lad. But it won't be easy."

Jerry had no misgivings, though. It would be a simple enough matter to climb into the partly emptied tank, slip to the bottom, and screw in the nipple. Once firmly fixed into the drain, they could feed the rockets from the safe tank, and have more time to work on the others.

He helped Tod with the welding. The filter was a big double-walled can of copper, with the space between the two metal layers filled with waste that would collect the lumps of tar. The holes in the metal of the cans would also keep some of the tar back, though they were not so fine that they could be covered over by the gummy lumps.

Probably after the tank reached the near-empty stage, the filter would clog up. But it should work long enough.

They loaded Jerry's pockets with lumps of metal—being sure that no tin was used—and went up to the tanks. Then Tod shook his head, and began unloading the metal from the suit. "Dumb fools! There's no weight."

Jerry grimaced, again aware of how easy it was to let habit overcome sounder thinking. Wtih gravity, a man sank in heavy liquid by adding weight—but here, everything weighed the same—exactly nothing!

The manhole presented a problem. It came loose easily enough, but the fuel immediately tried to spread out from it. It was thick enough to spread slowly, however. After a half dozen tries, followed by hasty moppings up, Jerry managed to get inside the tank almost as soon as the manhole was lifted. He held the filter and a wrench in one hand, and reached out for one of the tank walls with the other. Over him, Tod was screwing the manhole cover down firmly.

Now he was in complete darkness. The liquid of the fuel completely surrounded him, and it was so black that no light would have helped. He began to force his way to the bottom, using the rod that Tod had thrust down at the first opening.

The liquid was too thick. It was like trying to wade through thin molasses. With no weight to give him a sense of direction, he had to hope that he was heading for the bottom.

He felt the handholds, which should have lined the tank for the use of the crewmen who cleaned them. But he must have already been lost, since he couldn't locate one. From outside, it had seemed simple enough a matter to dive to the bottom at once. Now, it was an entirely different matter.

He began trying to swim through the stuff, and that was better. Progress was agonizingly slow, and each movement took more energy than it should, but he found that he could make some progress. He headed laboriously for what should have been the tank, but he wound up against another curved wall—he was still hugging the sides.

Half a dozen times he headed out from the wall toward where the bottom must be, only to find that he was still at the wall.

Finally, he began swimming around it, keeping in touch with it at the end of each stroke. It took a long time for his sense of direction to orient itself, but the curve of the wall finally guided him into a short, circular curve. The bottom had to be at right angles to that—or the top; there was no way of knowing which.

He came out at the top, judging by the fact that his fingers found the edge of the manhole. But it told him that the bottom must lie in the other direction, and he

was finally getting used to navigating in the little tank.
His sudden relief made him realize that he'd been half
panicky before.

Now he headed downward, and his direction was
right. The flatness of the bottom finally met his grop-
ing fingers. He swam along it, barely able to move his
arms. The long struggle through the thick stuff had
taken nearly all his strength, but he managed to keep
moving. He couldn't quit now.

Still touching the bottom, he circled the tank until he
could get the feel of where the center must be. Now he
moved out, feeling cautiously as he thought he must
have reached it. He was beginning to realize that locating a two-inch threaded hole in a tank of this size was
worse than finding a needle in any possible haystack.

Then his fingers noticed a change in the slope of the
floor; it was no longer completely flat, but seemed to
slope down. There must be a depression in the bottom,
leading to the drain. He followed it carefully.

His finger touched a rough edge, and found a small
hole. Kicking weakly with his legs to hold himself in
position, he brought the filter to it, and seated it. Once
in place, screwing it down was the matter of half a minute.

Jerry shook his head inside his helmet, and cautiously
lined himself up, before starting to swim for the top. He
was doing better, even though more slowly—he came
up directly under the manhole, to tap against it sharply.

It unscrewed quickly, and he felt Tod MacLane's
tough hands helping him out. The sound of the manhole
being closed reached him, and then light began to strike
his eyes as the engineer hastily cleaned off some of the
fuel from his helmet.

"What time?" he asked. Tod held up a watch, and he
was surprised to find that they still lacked half an hour
of his deadline. It had felt like fifty hours.

He wriggled out of his suit, stuffed the messy garment into a locker, and headed up the shaft.

He had to get the fuel off his hands before it could injure his skin. By then, Tod should have the fuel lines cleaned, with filtered fuel coming through, and Jerry belonged in the control room. He couldn't entirely trust his five-hour deadline.

CHAPTER 10 /

Distress Signal

JERRY was still unsure of how much danger they had been in, when he finally set the controls on automatic and climbed down the rail toward his hammock. It was in the past, anyhow, not worth worrying about. At least, they were out of danger now. He started to take off his worn uniform, but it was too much effort.

His body was a mass of aching muscles when he woke under Tod's urging. The engineer was shaking his shoulder and trying to tell him something. He groaned and sat up. Then he heard the buzz of the radio, and snapped out of his stupor. He even forgot the soreness of his muscles as he scrambled up the rail to the control room.

The signal in his headphones was the rasping buzz of an automatic signaler. "SOS! SOS! SOS!"

It went on endlessly. He tried to answer, but the signal was constant, with no interruptions, though its speed changed. It must be cranked by hand—and that meant the ship in distress was close.

He swept the vacuum with his radar antenna, watching for a telltale pip, while holding down the fixed response button so the screen would respond to anything, moving or not.

He found it, less than fifty miles away, and almost exactly matching his speed. Then he focused on it with the tele-panels, and saw that it was a sleek, long ship.

His hands cut the thrust of the rocket as he estimated their relative speeds. It was close enough for him to match course with it in a few minutes of juggling. He cut on the steering tubes, and swung delicately toward the other ship, drifting on without any flare from its rockets.

It was surprising to find how closely their courses matched. The other ship was a trifle faster than he was, and slightly off his course. A few touches of the main blast sent him drifting closer, until he was going a few miles per hour faster than they. More would require turning end over end and braking with the big tube. It would be quicker this way.

Tod muttered something, and pointed through the quartz ports, where the ship was now showing up plainly. "A Martian—and it looks like a racer. Must be the Martian ship!"

Jerry studied it, and nodded. It was clearly racing built. He'd thought that the Martians were days away before now, but there was no time to speculate. He could see a gaping hole, the size of a bathtub, in one wall. Evidently the ship had been struck a glancing blow by a meteorite, and a section of one wall had buckled in.

"Got a patch for that?" Jerry asked. Tod studied the size of the hole in the ship that was now only a few yards away, and nodded.

The *Last Hope* drew closer by the second now. Jerry studied the pattern of handholds on the skin of the Martian ship, and edged closer with the steering tubes. There was a shock and grating sound as the handholds on the *Last Hope* caught those of the other ship. Then it was over, and they were locked together loosely.

Jerry tried the radio again, but got no answer. He listened for a second. The SOS signals were still coming.

They must have felt the shock of contact, but were continuing to send so that he'd know they were still alive.

Tod came up from the engine room, bringing the welder and a rolled-up sheet of beryllium-aluminum alloy. He was half into his space suit, and he waited while Jerry climbed into the only other clean one.

Jerry followed Tod out through the air lock, carrying the welder. The other ship lay a few handholds away. Tod snapped on his rope, kicked off, and drifted to the other ship, grabbing a handhold, perhaps ten feet away from the gaping hole. Jerry swallowed nervously, but he followed Tod's example, and began pulling himself along the Martian ship until he could climb in through the hole. He was careful not to let the broken metal catch his suit. A puncture here meant almost immediate death.

Tod grinned briefly at him, and took the welder. The metal of the Martian ship was thin, as all racing hulls were, and the welder cut through it like a razor blade through paper. He cut away the rough edges in a few minutes, and began fitting the sheet he had brought over the hole.

Jerry held it while Tod tacked it in place with a few quick welds. The automatic machinery of the ship must still be working. A second later, there was a motion of air, and the ship began filling. The pressure forced the sheet firmly into place, and Tod sprayed the edges with a can of goo that would form a temporary seal.

Jerry pressed a flap on his helmet open and sampled the air. It was cold, but breatheable, and he threw the helmet back.

"Go look for the men," Tod told him. "I can tack this thing down in ten minutes."

Jerry found that the hole in the inner hull of the Martian ship was barely large enough for him to crawl through. He hadn't noticed it before, though he'd known it was there. The space between hulls was usually evacuated, and the air that flowed out had proved there must be a hole. The two facing walls were polished to a mirror finish that added to the insulating properties, and the outer hull stopped most of the tiny meteorites.

He crawled through into the unfamiliar maze of the Martian construction. It took him several minutes to find the railing between decks, located at the side of the vessel instead of down the center. He was beginning to worry now; the Martians should have come out, as soon as the air was sealed from escaping.

He worked his way up slowly to the front. When he found the main living quarters, the door was shut tightly, and the shock of the collision seemed to have sprung it. It refused to open until he braced his legs against one edge and pulled with his full strength. Then a gust of air almost knocked him down as it came open. Apparently, there had been a slow leak through the sprung door, but full pressure hadn't yet been reached.

The control room door was also sealed, but it opened now, bringing the smell of stale air. A stringy, tall Martian staggered out, breathing in great gulps of the pure air. Two others followed him.

"Thanks," the Martian captain said, finally, and a taut grin spread over his dark face. "Almost got us, before we spotted your blast. Didn't know whether you'd get the signal—our power was off up there."

Jerry could guess most of the story. They had apparently been forward when the collision came. The automatic doors had saved them, but the slow leak had finally forced them into the control room. Obviously, no suits had been near, and there had been no way for them to repair the damages. Then, after the hole was sealed, they'd had to wait until the outer quarters filled with air before they could open the control room seal.

"Down to our last bottle of canned air, when we saw you. For once, we're glad to see you, Earthman!"

Jerry grinned back, nodding. "And I'll have to admit I wasn't too sorry to see you here. I thought you'd be back to the inner planets by now. You had head start enough."

"Bad luck—ever since we reached Jupiter." The Martian shook his black-haired head bitterly. "The meteor finished it. Do you claim salvage?"

Jerry realized it was his right. They were almost back to the break now, and he saw Tod start to nod. Then the little man shrugged, made a face, and shook his head. Jerry agreed with him. In an emergency, even a man's worst enemy was entitled to any help that could be given. There had been cases of salvage claiming in such rescues, but it wasn't something looked on with any favor.

"You can fix the rest," he decided. "We've got to get back to the *Last Hope*. No salvage."

Even if they had caught up to the Martian, there were still six other ships to be beaten. Jerry had been forgetting them too long, taking it for granted that the Martian ship was his worst rival. Finding that they were neck and neck took some of the worry off him, but the race still had to go on.

He picked up his welder and reached for the snaps on his helmet. The Martian exchanged sudden glances with his two companions and raised a protesting hand.

"At least have a glass of zesto with us, Earthman. We have one bottle on board, and this is a good time to open it."

"They'll probably poison it," Tod warned sharply. But his eyes had a curious glitter. Zesto was a rare juice from a Martian herb. It wasn't a true stimulant, but it produced an almost miraculous power to make the body recover from fatigue, and the taste was delicious.

The Martian grinned thinly, without letting his hard face soften. "No poison. We take this race as a business; it is a business, since commerce thrives for the world that wins. You five billion Earthmen have all the advantages against our poor fifteen million. Perhaps we find strange ways to win—but the object is to win, not to embrace your neighbor! We do not kill, however!"

He seemed to be unusually talkative for a Martian. Jerry still hesitated, and the Martian went on. "You, young man, take all this like a sport. Win for dear old Earth! You're too proud to go around the rules, but you'll kill yourself and your crew in trying to win. We are businessmen—and businessmen know how to relax and not to try too hard—that leads only to errors in judgment, which is why you lose. You'll share the zest before we each blast off?"

Jerry looked inquiringly at Tod, who nodded slowly. There could be no harm in that, apparently. And there was just enough truth in the Martian's words to make them worth thinking over.

Maybe he had been trying too hard. Maybe the responsibility of knowing he was just a kid in a man's position had been getting him down. He was too conscious of being captain. He nodded doubtfully.

The Martian slapped his hand against a leather-covered thigh, and one of the men slipped off. He was back with a little green bottle and five paper cups. "Choose your cups, and pour first," the Martian suggested.

Jerry started to refuse such a precaution against poison, but Tod was already pouring. He filled two cups, and handed one to Jerry. The Martians filled their own.

"Your health—and our success!"

"Darn all Martians!" Tod said flatly. The Martians laughed shortly, and lifted the cups. Jerry swallowed his slowly, letting it trickle down.

Almost immediately, the fatigue and soreness seemed to leave his body. It would have been a dangerous relaxation, except for the fact that the herb extract actually did improve the general tone of the body.

Now the Martian captain glanced at a wrist watch, and seemed all business again. "Thank you for the rescue," he stated formally.

Jerry put down his cup, and again reached for his helmet clasps. "Thanks for the zesto," he replied. Then he snapped the helmet closed and began heading toward the air lock the Martian was opening.

The outer seal of the lock opened automatically. Jerry found that they were less then two feet above one of the handholds of the *Last Hope*. He reached for it and began moving carefully along the shell of his ship, heading for his own air lock. Unlike alcohol, the zesto produced no false feeling of confidence. He was careful to keep himself snapped to the handholds by the ropes and clamps on his belt as he moved along. The sound of Tod behind him reached him through the metal of the ship.

He glanced back, to see that two of the Martians were in the air lock of their ship, pushing against the *Last Hope* with metal poles. Inertia still made it hard to move large bodies, even without weight, but the two ships were beginning to drift apart now. The Martians waited until the poles would no longer reach, and then closed their outer lock.

Jerry slipped cautiously into the lock of the *Last Hope* and helped Tod in. They shucked off the space suits as quickly as they could, and went up to the control room. Tod was still frowning doubtfully.

"We should have let them rot out here," he complained. "It doesn't pay to help Martians!"

"Maybe that's what's wrong with the whole affair. Maybe if we helped them more, they'd stop pulling foul play on us," Jerry suggested. Tod made no answer, but he still stared suspiciously out at the Martian ship.

It was maneuvering off cautiously with its steering rockets now, waiting for space enough to enable the ships to use their main blasts without danger to each other. Jerry began sliding the *Last Hope* away with equal care. Now a few hundred feet separated the two ships.

"They couldn't hurt us this time, anyhow," he

pointed out to Tod. "We had them all under our eyes. You can't desert a damaged ship out here."

Tod agreed sourly. "You did the right thing, lad. I'm not saying you didn't. But you still can't trust them."

Jerry let him fume. He was probably ready to believe that the Martians had deliberately wrecked their ship and holed themselves up just to slow down the *Last Hope*.

"They got power in the control room awful fast," Tod pointed out suddenly. "Less than five minutes after we leave, they can work the steering rockets. I thought they didn't have enough current to work a radio."

He had a point there, though Jerry couldn't see what good it could have done the Martians to go through any elaborate pretense.

Now the Martian ship belched out a thin streak of deep violet exhaust, and began moving off rapidly. Surprisingly, it seemed to be pointing back toward Jupiter, to intercept Callisto or Ganymede at the side of the big planet.

"Maybe they're hurt worse than they thought," he muttered.

"Take another look," Tod snorted. The old engineer was shaking his fists at the retreating ship, hopping about in sudden fury that sent him in great jumps from the ceiling to the floor. He extended a finger, pointing. "Look at that blast!"

Jerry tightened his fists into hard knots as it hit him. The racing rocket from Mars was using a red blast— and this was uncolored! It couldn't have been the racer. It must have been another Martian ship, fixed up to look like a racer, and waiting out here to intercept him.

He let his mind race back over the words he'd exchanged with the other captain. The Martian had never said that he was in the race. He'd told no lies, but had let Jerry leap to his own conclusions.

But he could still see no sense to it. The delay had been only for half an hour, and it wasn't worth all that trouble. He should have been suspicious at the strange similarity of their speeds and courses, but such things had happened before.

Then he stopped, staring at Tod. "We saw three of them—but we wouldn't have known if there'd been a fourth one in a space suit. And we left the *Last Hope* wide open. Tod, that Martian didn't want us to leave too fast—that's why he offered us the zesto!"

Tod let out an agonized cry and jumped for the rail to rush down to inspect his engines. Jerry checked over the control panel rapidly. There seemed to be nothing wrong. A moment later, Tod's voice came over the phone.

"Nothing here—the fuel spray we couldn't swab up before got all over the floor when you put on thrust. I can see my footprints, but there ain't any others. How about you?"

"We'll soon see." Jerry cut on the blast. It responded perfectly, as the little steering rockets had done before. He checked over his instruments and found them responding properly. Nothing seemed to be disturbed.

He set the ship back on automatic course, reporting to Tod. The engineer muttered something under his breath. Then he snorted. "Don't worry, lad. We'll find out soon enough what the dirty crooks were up to!"

Jerry didn't answer. He was staring at his chart rack, and he already knew what had been taken. The asteroid chart was missing—the one chart that he'd have to have within the next few hours. Without it, it was almost suicide to try to run through the crazy belt of rocks and rubble and grinding planetoids.

But he had to go through or quit the race.

CHAPTER 11 /

Smallpox of Space

THE asteroid belt was the roughest section in the Solar System, and only fools and ignorant men went through it, according to the books. The fools were the rocket racers, of course. And the miners who prospected the little hunks of rock and metal were mostly ignorant. Even their names for themselves showed that. Scientists had repeatedly pointed out that they couldn't mine meteors, which were only the disturbance caused by a meteorite striking an atmosphere. They should have been called meteorite miners, of course; but they were used to referring to themselves as meteor miners, and the name stuck.

Even they were not foolish enough to try to cut through the belt at millions of miles per hour. They took it in short hops, at safe speeds, and they knew the section where they worked.

Once, so astronomers believed, there had been a planet between Mars and Jupiter. Then Jupiter's pull had broken it up, and the pieces had been broken into smaller fragments, until now there were millions of rocky bits circling there in crazy, twisted orbits. Some were no bigger than pebbles, but others were tiny worlds, miles in diameter. Several thousand of the larger ones had been spotted before men ever reached the Moon.

Jerry had spent his time working on the radar spotting device, trying to increase its sensitivity enough to make it useful at the speed with which they were traveling. He'd pored over the section they would hit in his mind, wracking his memory for the orbits of all the larger ones.

But he knew it was hopeless to trust to memory. The belt became thicker at three hundred million miles from the sun, and went on until it finally petered out at a little over two hundred million miles. In all that space, it was impossible to guess accurately where there would be danger of a collision.

Surprisingly, Tod was less worried than he was. The engineer had grown up in the belt and had rarely left it. To him, the hunks of rock and broken little worlds were familiar things; they were dangerous, of course—but only to men who didn't know what they were doing.

He grumbled impatiently at Jerry. "If you're going to get scared now, then pull out. Go over the belt, like the freighters do. Tell the Commission you lost your chart! Dadgum it, you *know* the belt!"

"Not at millions of miles an hour," Jerry answered.

"But you're just getting scared because you've been listening to all that fancy school talk. I've read some of the books—make it seem like there's a rock every ten feet." He caught his breath, swallowing his Venus gum. For a second, it stopped him. Then he blinked and went on. "You know durned well you don't find a rock every hundred miles—or every thousand, for that matter!"

Jerry let him fume. He knew that it would take only one, and that a lot of former racers had died there, even at much slower speeds, and with good charts.

But he had grown determined that nothing would make him give up. After the last incident with Mars, he meant to finish, if it took a year. And he didn't intend to be the last one in. Mars might win, but she wasn't going to have a complete laugh at Earth.

He'd slept a full ten hours before they began to get pips on the radar screen, and now he was refreshed enough. There was only the feeling of strain to cloud his reactions. He had the foot pedals out, controlling one bank of steering rockets and the main drive. His hands rested on the other steering controls. And his eyes were fixed on the radar screen.

Tod gave up, finally. Probably he'd been thinking over the effect of a ship colliding with anything at their speed, and had begun to get worried. He went below, grumbling to himself. This time Jerry was glad to see him leave. He'd need every bit of his energy to concentrate on the belt.

At a guess, there was one chance in forty that they could sail straight through without actually hitting anything big enough to do any damage. But that was too much to expect.

All he could do was to hope that his memory hadn't played him false, and that the section into which he was heading was the thinnest. It brought him off his course a bit, but that couldn't be helped.

He began to notice more pips now. The screen was adjusted so that the nearer bits would register more brightly than the others. Size was less important, since a good-sized pebble could wreck the ship now. They were covering almost two thousand miles every second.

The radar had a calculator, designed to predict the course of the meteorites and register in red all those offering danger. But Jerry couldn't count on it's working at the speed they were making; there was no time for plotting courses properly.

In this crisis, he'd had to drop back on the oldest of all instruments—his human mind, with its ability to put a hundred half-facts together to arrive at an almost instant answer. It could make mistakes, but at least it would give some answers.

A bright red flashed on the screen, and he kicked down on the steering controls, then hit the main drive to nearly three gees for a split second as he saw a glare of white. It should have been safe, according to the screen, but it had felt wrong to him. He was counting on hunches now—hunches that had been trained in this same belt.

He could never know whether his action saved them or whether they'd have missed anyhow. But he missed.

His mind seemed to detach itself from the rest of him, leaving a machine at the keys, jerking the *Last Hope* about savagely at the whim of the lights on the screen. Sam Hoadley had run the belt once, he remembered, with his sick wife—straight through from Io to Mars, without a scratch; and the old-timer hadn't even know how to read a chart. It could be done. But he knew that was a freak trick.

Then the first patch was over. There were spots in the belt where the pulls of Jupiter and Mars had swept space fairly clean. He found Tod standing beside him, holding a plastic can of coffee, and he gulped it down, letting the old man handle it while he kept his hands on the controls.

A few minutes later, they were in the thick of it again. Lights flashed warning, and his fingers moved. Tod dropped into a seat, buckling in against the pitching of the ship, but kept silent.

A sudden clear lane showed on the screen, and he hit the controls to make the tiny change that would bring them into it. The few yards difference the steering rockets made in his course wouldn't have been noticeable to anyone watching him from a few thousand miles away, but here they meant the difference between life and death.

Something clipped against the ship, with the sound of a thousand mad Oriental demons, all in a hundredth of a second. Tod got up, but Jerry didn't dare to glance around. The old man was back a minute later.

"Tiny one. Cut through the outer hull, but missed the inner one—must have gone out through the tail. No leaks."

He heard it without letting his mind relax from the screen and the controls. At the speed they were making, the motion of the rocks out there really didn't count— everything would seem almost like a straight head-on collision with a motionless body.

That brought the chances up, he tried to tell himself. There was one chance in twelve of getting by with only a single hit from a small meteorite. But he knew that it might be good statistics and still have no meaning; getting hit once was no assurance of not being hit again; in fact, it helped to prove that his mind and the screen were subject to failure.

The fairly clear sections were all that saved him. They gave him a chance to catch his breath, relax for a few seconds, and rub the tension out of his muscles.

He was amazed to find that they'd already covered half the distance, and that he'd been sitting there for over six hours.

Then it began again, but it was a little thinner now, and his memory indicated that the path ahead was freer than most. The screen seemed to confirm it.

He began to hope, until three red dots glared up, almost at once. He hit the controls, without knowing what he was doing, consciously.

Something flicked across the port ahead, big and almost touching, but gone before his eyes could really see it. Tod gasped and ducked instinctively, though it could do no good here.

"When you see them, forget them," Jerry said. It was one of Tod's own favorite comments on random meteorites in the belt. The old man chuckled, but it was a feeble sound.

Jerry's mind wandered off again, while half of it stayed frozen to the controls. He should be turning over now, if he was to brake down toward Venus. But how could he turn over in this crazy mass of rocks?

His stomach muscles were sore from the strapping that held him to the seat. Each jerk of the ship was beginning to feel like an evil hand that clutched at his nerves. But he couldn't let up to favor it.

The tension was beginning to mount now. They were coming toward the end of the main part of the belt. They'd escaped so far. But the feeling that it would wait until the last minute and then strike grew stronger in him. It was simply fear and dread, he knew. It was totally illogical. But he couldn't put it down.

They should have worn space suits. Then if one drilled a hole through the ship, they could at least have a faint chance. But it was too late to put them on now—he couldn't take time.

Tod jumped up suddenly, half an hour later, and opened a chest. He took out some little things that looked like balloons and released them. They floated in the air, bobbing around, but they got in the way. The engineer began chasing them, catching them by short strings that dangled from them. Jerry shouted in annoyance.

Then the old man was sitting down, holding them by the strings. Jerry forgot them. They passed through the last cleared section, and then into the final area of danger.

Something cracked sharply at the quartz port in front of him, and a tremendous scream went by his ear, with a blaze of heat and a shock wave of air that threw him out of the seat, straps and all. There was a horrible bursting sound down the central shaft, and more heat came welling up.

Jerry had time for only the single thought that this was it, before blackness squeezed down on his mind.

He came out of it to find Tod just pushing up from the floor. It was still hot, and the air stank of burned metal, but the air was apparently no thinner. He must have been unconscious for a few minutes at most.

He sat up, testing for broken bones. The violence of the shock waves had made him a solid mass of aching flesh, but he could still move. He turned toward Tod, but the old man was getting to his feet.

"We're tough." His voice trembled faintly in Jerry's ears, but it steadied almost at once. "I'm all right. How about you, kid?"

Jerry nodded, unable to speak. He stared at the port, where a tiny hole the size of a pea showed. And finally he understood the purpose of the little balloons. The air must have begun to rush out just as they escaped from Tod's hand. They'd floated in the air currents, to jam up against the hole and break, releasing their small loads of quick-hardening goo. The hole was sealed.

Jerry glanced at the screen and was amazed that no damage seemed to have been done his instruments. It looked clear. They'd gotten through the belt, still alive. If the ship wasn't permanently damaged, they were out of the danger.

He hobbled after Tod, crawling down the rail. The tiny meteorite had cracked through the port and hit the air with a speed that had turned the atmosphere in the ship into a solid wall in front of it—unable to get out of its way. It had driven that seemingly solid air back by sheer force, changing its speed to heat as it went, until it had finally volatilized completely. There was no trace of it left.

At that speed, it hadn't mattered whether it hit air or a wall of solid iron—the results would have been about the same.

The shock wave in the central shaft had obviously been terrific. The tube was buckled in one place, and the rail was bent.

"No bigger than a pea," Tod said slowly. "Just a speck!"

"If it had been bigger, we'd be nothing but spots of

grease, Tod. After that, I'm done calling this a jinx ship. We've had our share of good luck for the whole race, right here!"

If the engines aren't hurt," Tod amended it. He pulled himself down the rail. Jerry started to follow, but it wasn't worth the work. He crawled back into the control room. The phone weighed a ton in his hand as he waited for Tod's report.

But apparently everything was all right. Jerry took the controls again in fingers that seemed to be without feeling, and began turning the ship end for end, to begin killing their wild speed—probably greater than any rocket ship had ever reached before. The steering tubes behaved perfectly. He swung the tail down to point toward the sun, steadied it, and set the ship back on an automatic course.

There was still some danger of striking a meteorite; there was always that possibility in space, where a few bits of rock or metal danced around the sun in wild, elliptical orbits. But it was no more than normal, and that was one of the least of their dangers.

Tod came clumping slowly up the rail, and nodded as he saw that they were decelerating at last. But his face was grim.

"Broke a lead plate over the exciter for the tube," he reported. "Must have been brittle, anyhow, but that finished it."

The ship was still operating, though. Jerry had never had time to learn all about his father's fuel, and he groped back in his memory. There had been something about using one of the tiny atom-cracking machines to trigger the fuel into exploding, he remembered now. It must be the hood-shaped gadget at the end of the big rocket tube.

"Will it last till we land?" he asked.

Tod nodded. "It'll last. But it means we stay out of the engine room as much as we can. There's radio-activity escaping now, and it won't be healthy. Maybe it's all right—takes a certain amount of that to do any damage. But we don't have any way of testing what's safe and what isn't."

Jerry considered it. They'd already filtered the fuel in the other tanks, pumping from full tank to empty one as soon as the first one was used up.

"Then we'll have to stay out of there. If nothing else goes wrong, we can get it fixed on Mercury, maybe."

"Mercury? Lad, they've got better shops on Venus, where we're bound." Tod looked at the hastily drawn course, and back again to Jerry. "What's the idea of changing to Mercury?"

Jerry handed over his quick figures, made from a hasty check of their position. The answer was plain enough.

Again, they'd come too far before being able to turn over to decelerate. No thrust they could safely pile on would stop them at Venus' orbit. But Mercury lay thirty million miles nearer to the sun, and they could reach that planet safely, unless his figures were all wrong. At this stage, there wasn't much point in trying to follow Dick's original plan, since they were days behind, and all the planetary positions were slightly different.

Tod handed the paper back.

"No decent shops on Mercury. We'll be lucky to get any kind of repair work there. But you're the captain, lad—and I guess I can't argue with your figuring. Hit the sack!"

"We both hit it, this time," Jerry told him.

The old man didn't protest. Neither one of them could have sat upright for ten minutes more. And there wasn't much they could do now, anyhow.

Tod made no comment as Jerry flopped onto the hammock in his clothes. The old man reached for his shoes, hesitated, and then climbed into his own hammock fully dressed.

CHAPTER 12 /

The Burning Planet

Tod was partly wrong about the shops on Mercury. There were shops, Jerry discovered over the radio—but they were of limited capability. They could do routine repairs, but on such tricky equipment as many of the racers carried, they were of no help. They offered to beat the lead plate back into shape, until Tod explained. Then they gave up.

The lead had crystallized and become brittle under the bombardment of nuclear particles inside the little atom-cracker, and it was also radioactive itself on its inner surfaces. They'd have to have an entirely new plate made.

Jerry still found it hard to believe that the little world could support life at all. Smaller than Mars, it circled the sun at only thirty-six million miles out, making a complete circle every eighty-eight days. One side was always pointed toward the sun, and the temperature there rose to over seven hundred degrees—hot enough to make rivers of tin and lead flow easily! The other side was frozen and dark.

The little colonies were all along the twilight belt, where a dangerous living was possible. Mercury wobbled a bit, so that every eighty-eight days the little colo-

nies went through a single change from sunset to sunrise
and back. They hovered there, between incredible heat
and intense cold. There was no air, of course.

Jerry set the ship down while there was still just a
touch of dawn near the little dome. The colony couldn't
have held more than five hundred people, and all of
them were out to see him land on the tiny little field.
They had brought with them a big platform on wheels,
with a tiny dome over it.

Jerry landed at eight P.M., Sunday the twenty-second,
by the ship's clock. After the last long stretch—just two
hours less than six days—any planet would have looked
good to him.

He went out in his space suit, to be met by a crowd
that leaped around him, thumping him on the back, and
touching helmets to yell questions. He'd never seen so
many completely natural smiles in his life. They led him
into the domed platform, and he found that it was a
hastily contrived device to give him a small enclosed
hall!

The local representative of the Commission turned
out to be the mayor of the colony, a young man of
about thirty. The coveralls that seemed to be their universal garment were all of dull gray, but the mayor had
ornamented his by sewing on a white badge of some
strange material, with the symbol of the Commission
sketched onto it.

He signed the papers, and threw them back. "From
one fool to another—you race rockets, I live in this for-
saken hole! You'd like it here, if you ever care to settle
down."

Jerry found himself grinning. He'd heard the legends
of the happy-go-lucky, scatterbrained Mercutians, but
seeing them was different. Probably the legends were
true; they were all hopeless gamblers, who got no satisfaction out of anything except the daily gamble for their
lives that this represented.

But they were neat and clean, and the little dome

looked as if it might be comfortable. He even saw flowers blooming inside it, the first ones he'd seen since leaving Earth.

They knew nothing definite about the race. Mars was winning, of course; they took that for granted. It didn't matter to them. Their own entry hadn't arrived yet—probably gotten himself killed trying to touch Saturn, too! They said it with a grin, but Jerry wouldn't have put it past anyone who came from here.

Then he found why he'd received such a cordial welcome. Io had finally spread the word of his dive into Jupiter, and he was automatically one of them.

Some of them were helping Tod load the ship, while the others talked to Jerry. He saw them making a game of it, tossing the big cans of fuel about carelessly. It looked as if they were doing nothing but waste time, yet the loading seemed to be going on well enough.

Finally the mayor got down to business. "I hear you've got a little radioactivity running loose?"

"Some," Jerry admitted, trying to fit into their crazy way of looking at things. "Probably about enough to kill a man."

The mayor picked up a small Geiger counter, zipped up his helmet, and motioned Jerry with him. Two of the children tried to follow him, but he chased them back. "And you'd better stay well behind me, too," he warned Jerry. "No use getting a burn, if you're still trying to beat Mars."

"What about you?" Jerry wanted to know. There was no sign of lead shielding to protect him in the simple coveralls he wore.

"Me—I'm radiation immune." He saw Jerry's doubtful expression, and nodded emphatically. "It's a fact. The scientists have found a few of us. Me, I found it out when I lost a bet and had to get a guy out of an explosion, back on Earth. Stuff killed him, but it never touched me."

He swung out and up the ladder into the *Last Hope,*

with Jerry behind him. In the ship, he moved down the shaft and was gone a few minutes. He came back shaking his head.

"Enough there to kill a man in a day, I'd say. Good thing you two stayed out of there. Mostly alpha particles, of course, but it's not good medicine. You can't go on without a new plate."

Tod had come in, and he listened to the verdict glumly. He already knew that Mercury had no supplies of lead. If it meant running on to Venus without a man in the engine room, anything might happen. They'd already left things alone much too long.

"What's all the stuff about lead in rivers out there?" he asked, pointing out toward the hot side of the planet. "Don't you ever collect any of that?"

"Too far out," the mayor answered. "And we don't need lead here. We go in for the precious stuff that's close by. If we didn't, we'd never be able to afford the prices you Earthmen charged us for building those three racers for us! The tractors can't work out far enough to find molten lead."

"Do you know where there is any?" Jerry asked.

He nodded. "Sure. There's a whole lake of it about three hundred miles from here. I've seen it from the sky when I crossed to the domes on the other side, and it doesn't look like tin to me. Must be lead."

The idea that had crossed Jerry's mind seemed too fantastic, and yet Tod was nodding at him. "You're as crazy as I am," he told his engineer.

The old man chuckled. "We need lead, and there's plenty of it out there. Think we can rig a scoop of some sort onto the *Last Hope?*"

Maybe it was catching, he thought. Either he'd caught the nonsense from the mayor, or else the things that had happened had dulled his sense of caution. Apparently, for once, it had affected Tod the same way.

"Take a couple hours," the engineer answered.

The mayor cocked his head at them, and his grin

broadened. "Looks like you two men are applying for citizenship here. Or burial. You're crazy enough to pass. Come on out to the shack."

In the little portable dome, he explained the idea to some of the men. There was some discussion of the impurity of the lead they'd find—it would dissolve other metals, of course. But that didn't matter for their purposes. In the back of the little dome, a group of them began drawing cards out of a deck. The mayor went back, and chose one. He and another man held up aces.

"Looks like you've got your scoops, boys," he told the two Earthmen. "Me—and this poor character. Wait'll we get our heavy suits and some hot side tackle to fasten on with, and we'll go for a ride."

The two men slipped out before Jerry could fully realize that they were volunteering to ride outside the *Last Hope* and drag up the lead in buckets somehow. He had heard no discussion of it. They seemed to act as a single man.

When they came back, they were dressed in big metal outfits, something like the old pictures of space suits he'd seen in a museum. The metal gleamed brightly, and from its thickness he knew it must be heavily insulated against the heat. Big metal-mesh straps were fastened to the suits.

Jerry tried to protest, but they signaled that they couldn't hear. One of the men handed him a small case and plugged it into the suits.

The mayor's voice came out of the instrument, "Well, you ready?"

Jerry repeated his protests. This wasn't like piloting a rocket in space—it meant fighting against the pull of gravity where only a few feet might spell disaster, and where it would require constant effort to keep upright. In the ship, they would be fairly safe; the big tube would kick any molten metal out of the way, if they turned it on full blast. But the men on the outside had no chance, in such a case. Also, they'd be slapped around too roughly if full acceleration had to be used.

"Can't hear a thing," the mayor stated. "You ready?"

He was swinging a huge metal pan that was attached to a long length of metal rope, and there was a block and tackle affair on his belt. He grinned impudently out of the thick helmet and swung out toward the ship.

Other men sprang to buckle him to the handholds, lacing his back down against the ship, and fastening the block and tackle affair to other grips. The second man was receiving the same treatment on the other side. The wire from the big suit was strung up expertly along the side, and up to the control room, leaving the communication box in front of the pilot's seat. At the port, they'd cut it and installed a small gadget on each side, to relay the sound through the quartz.

Tod sat down beside Jerry. "The durned fools want to do it," he said. "They're all crazy here!"

"Absolutely. But think of the fun we'll have bragging about it to our grandchildren after we get out," the mayor's voice said from the box.

"If you get out," Jerry amended it. He was sick of the whole thing now. It struck him as a senseless risk of men's lives, and he began to wonder how anybody managed to live for more than a few days here. Probably, though, it took men with a complete lack of fear and sense to get by out in the hotlands on the tiny tractors.

The crowd outside seemed happy about the whole thing. He reached out reluctantly and threw power into the big rocket, lifting upward as gently as he could. From the box, a baritone voice began singing: "Rock-a-bye baby, on the ship's side, when the kid shakes, the rocket will slide, when the kid breaks, the rocket will drop . . ."

Jerry grunted and hit the control a little harder.

"Woops," the voice commented. "Rough sea. That all the power this can handles?"

He gave up. They could needle him better than he could hand back. He followed their directions, heading upward in a long parabola, and drifting back down. So far, everything had been easy. Below him, the lake they had mentioned appeared, with a thick scum over part of it. Where it was clear, it looked like a mirror, except for the glowing red of the shores around it. He lowered carefully. Somehow, it wouldn't have seemed so hard to settle, if he'd meant to land. But knowing he was balancing indefinitely made it tough.

The ship swayed a little, and he corrected it with gentle taps of the side rockets. It came down until the big blast seemed to be touching the surface.

"Down fifty feet and hold her," the voice from the box ordered. Jerry eased down slowly, hoping he could hold the ship up without having to use flame enough from the rocket to splash metal up at them.

"Woops, up a bit—good boy." The words were light enough, but the voice was serious now. "You okay, Jake? Get your shovel down. It won't sink in lead, but see if you can—right, hold it on edge. Kid!"

"Right," Jerry answered.

"Give her tail a quick twist north. Gotta jerk these scoops into the stuff."

Jerry hesitated, trying to figure out a way of kicking on the side rockets without tilting the ship. There was none. He hit the steering controls sharply, and cut them off at once. The ship jerked, and he threw in the big rocket and began lifting as he straightened out.

The mayor's voice sounded quite happy, between the jerks as the erratic motion of the ship cut off his speech. "Beat you, Jake. I got a full scoop. Oof! This stuff weighs, even with the tackle. Okay, kid, go on home."

Jerry mopped the sweat from his face. The lake of lead looked peaceful and calm as he rose higher. Jake, who had been silent, began to discuss the idea of changing some of their little ships over for metal fishing. Apparently their only reaction to it all was that it was less fun than tractor mining—safe enough for old women—

but faster. "Get a couple of grapple poles on the outside, and we'd rake in a fortune, Bill."

The mayor seemed to think the same. Jerry wasn't sure whether they were kidding him or whether they really meant it. For all he knew, tractor mining might very well be more dangerous. The surface of Mercury looked evil enough to make it seem quite probable.

He came down smoothly on the little rocket field again, careful to set down without more than a faint bump. He didn't want to seem any more of an amateur then he had to before these men.

They were being unfastened as he came down the ladder, and were heading into the portable dome, to change back to their normal lightweight space clothes. Jerry saw that there was more than enough lead in the two scoops. It had cooled on the return trip, and looked solid now, though he knew it was still too hot to touch.

Tod seemed to have lost his voice somewhere out there. The old man had always considered the miners in the asteroids to be the roughest and toughest men alive, but these crazy fools made the meteor miners seem almost tame.

The mayor went back into the ship, to return with the cracked plate. Even under the quarter gravity pull of Mercury, the plate was all he could carry, but he obviously considered it his job. As one of the almost mythical men who seemed to be able to repair his tissues faster than radiation could harm them, he was the logical man for it, too.

Tod went along to supervise the casting of a new plate, using the old one for a mold. It was routine work for any shop, of course, even the makeshift one here. Jerry tried to pry more information about the race out of the people, but without any luck. He knew he'd be better off for not knowing, but he couldn't keep from trying to discover how far behind he was.

They apparently didn't know anything more than he did. The planet was so close to the sun that solar radiation played havoc with the beamed interplanet radio communications, and they only got snatches most of the time. He found that five of the ships had already touched Mercury, but he had no way of knowing whether it was on the last lap or the first.

Several of the men brought back the new plate later, but again it was the mayor who carried it down into the engine room and placed it in position. He came up for the Geiger counter, went back, and reported that it was safe now. The alpha rays were unlike neutrons; they created very little secondary radioactivity in the material they struck.

Tod seemed satisfied with their ability. He let the men shoo him away, and joined Jerry in the dome, where a rude meal was prepared. The food was rough and simple, though well prepared. But after the steady diet from cans, it tasted good to them.

They were finished when the mayor returned. "Reckon you two will be shoving straight off," he told them. "Drop in again sometime. We've had more fun than a barrel of monkeys. And that new idea of mining may come in handy."

There was no formality, but the whole crowd stood by as Jerry lifted the ship again, just eight hours after the landing. They'd made much better time in getting repairs than he had hoped for.

Tod shook his head at the crazy world below. "You know, lad," he announced, "maybe I will go back there some time."

Jerry grinned. He'd been thinking the same.

CHAPTER 13 /

Council of War

INSTINCTIVELY, Jerry looked for Venus. It lay in an orbit that was only thirty-one million miles beyond that of Mercury, and it should have been easily visible against the black of space. But there was no sign of it.

Then he realized he was making another mistake out of sheer habit of thought. Even more than two centuries after the beginning of space travel, men automatically thought of the planets as being straight out from the sun. He knew Venus was now approaching the opposite side of old Sol from that of Mercury.

He checked it against the charts, and located it. Then he whistled. It was almost exactly across the face of the sun from him—the hardest place of all to reach. It meant he'd have to go out in a great circle, constantly changing the angle of the big rocket, to cut around the sun and come up on the planet from behind. Instead of a mere thirty million miles, it would be closer to a hundred million—and he'd never be able to build up full speed, because of the circular course he'd have to take.

It would all be easy enough, if the sun weren't right in the way. Then he could cut across. He might even make up a little of the lost time from Dick's schedule. As it was, he'd lose at least another full day.

He tried to convince himself that he could afford the extra day, but he knew he didn't believe it. Dick had figured on an impossibly tight schedule of less than nineteen days—but he'd been right in saying that each Classic broke the record set by the last one. Jerry knew he was probably only fooling himself in thinking he still had any chance. An extra day of lost time would almost surely prove fatal.

He began figuring new orbits frantically, but the best he could do wasn't good enough. He picked up the phone and called for Tod to come up. This time he wasn't going to try anything foolish without finding out the facts and getting the old engineer's consent.

"Tod," he asked, "how close can we shave the sun?"

Tod screwed up his face and picked the paper off a new stick of Venus gum. He scowled as he got it working. "I dunno, lad. Maybe we can take it as close as fifteen million miles."

It was worse than Dick's stories of pilots had led Jerry to believe. "But didn't Tom Malone get down to about six million miles?"

"Yep. And when they boarded his ship on the other side, the instrument records were right useful to the scientists, I guess. Tom left a nice young widow, I understand."

"But men have come closer to the sun than fifteen million miles and lived," Jerry insisted.

"A lot closer. They've got sun-shields now—stuff that costs six fortunes and a government budget, but really throws back the heat. Get too close, and you'll melt the hide off this ship, Jerry. Mercury got kind of hot, but she's a lot farther away."

Yeah, Jerry thought. It would have been nice to have the sun-shields; he'd been taught that men had been within three million miles of the surface of the sun and come through—though he preferred Tod's accounts to what he remembered from the books.

He threw down his orbits in disgust. They had to skirt closer than he dared if they were to save any real time on this leg of the trip. In Dick's original orbit, they had expected to make the jump from Venus to Mercury more than four days earlier, when conditions were somewhat more favorable.

He began figuring again. They'd be making a speed of close to four million miles an hour when they came opposite the sun, counting on the pull of the sun plus every bit of energy they could safely squeeze from the rocket. He calculated the length of time carefully from different distances. There'd be only a short period when they were directly beside the sun.

The other men hadn't been equipped with a fuel that could handle such power or build up such speeds. It was the one factor in the whole race that was on his side, and he wanted to make use of that speed whenever he could.

"Suppose we were to move from about twelve million miles to five and out to twelve again in less than three hours—could we take that, Tod?"

The engineer shrugged his shoulders. "I don't know, Jerry. Honest I don't. You'd probably melt down one side of the ship, though. Look, you're the captain here. After what we've been through, and after those fools on Mercury, I don't much care what you figure up!"

He went down to the galley, where Jerry heard him trying to prepare a meal that would be different but ready to cook when they were hungry. Tod seemed as fond of experimenting in the galley as he was of crooning over the engines.

But it left things squarely up to Jerry. He consulted the handbook of engineering and the one on navigation, but they gave him little help.

With the best calculation he could make, the result

would be about what Tod had suggested; they'd simply melt off the hull on one side of the ship.

It made a beautiful orbit, though. They could have headed close to the sun, using the immense pull of that start to add to their speed. It would turn their course without any help from constant corrections—just as a rope tied to a stake will force a lunging dog to turn aside. By the time they began to pull away, they'd be on a course headed almost exactly for where Venus would be. And the total time would be little more than heading straight across, if there had been no sun. It would even take less time than Dick had allowed for the run from Venus to Mercury.

But there was no point in destroying the ship, or in raising the inside temperature so high that they'd be cooked.

There had to be some way. No other course gave them the same advantage of not having to force themselves into a circle of awkward size and hard maneuvering.

"We could spin the ship," Tod shouted up, suddenly. "Help some, though you'd have a deuce of a time doing any steering."

Dick had always spoken with contempt of men who let their ships get into a spin—but it would keep one side from overheating. Effectively, it would cut the heating effect in half.

He tried to imagine steering from a rotating ship, but it was something that would have to be tried. He could see that it wouldn't be easy.

But it still didn't solve the problem of overheating inside the ship. A vacuum and metallic reflectors inside the walls provided the most nearly perfect insulation possible, outside of the impossible sun-shields. There was no way of improving on that.

The ship had some degree of refrigeration, of course—without it, there would have been enough heat from the big rocket to cook them slowly. But it couldn't be raised too far; perhaps it could take care of a hundred extra degrees, but no more.

Then Jerry thought of the refrigeration devices built into the space suits to cool them, or by reversing the controls, to warm them. The suits could stand a fairly high temperature without letting a man roast. They could wear the suits inside during the critical period.

He called Tod up again, and began reeling off his new ideas. He expected the man to turn them down, but the engineer shook his head in slow thought.

"I dunno. Maybe it could be done, for a short while, like you say, Jerry. I just don't know. You must want to win this race pretty bad for a boy who didn't want to come along!"

Jerry hadn't realized how much he did want to win, but he nodded. It was a host of things—Dick sick on Mars and counting on him, the tricks Mars had pulled, the feeling that this was his chance to prove himself a man and old Commodore Tenn a fool—a thousand things, including the remarks of the false Martian captain. The Classic would only go on stirring up hatred between the planets as long as it could be won by underhanded tricks. But if it could be won fairly by superior equipment, some of that hatred might die down.

"Are you willing to try it?" he asked the old man.

Tod chewed thoughtfully. "I reckon so, Jerry. I don't say I'm going to like it, but I'll ride along with you. No place else to go, anyhow. Let her rip!"

It wasn't that simple. Jerry had to refine his calculations down to the closest possible course he could figure, and to be sure of his fix. He began setting it up, trying to take everything into account this time.

"Food's going to be spoiled," Tod told him. "Heat will cook it for sure. You'll have broken cans all over the place, bust from the heat."

It didn't matter. They could get new food on Venus, and there was enough dry stuff to live on until they got there—or they could go hungry, for that matter.

"How much water do we have?" he asked, as the calculator clicked along with his figures.

"Couple hundred gallons. Oh! Blow it out into space, eh—let it boil and use up some of the heat, if we have to?" Tod grinned. "We can do the same with some of the fuel; we got more than we need. And then there's the oxygen in the tanks. That'll soak up some heat. I'd better get set to have pipes out to the hull to use it."

He hopped down the shaft, while the calculations came out slowly. But they checked with Jerry's original rough figures. With luck, they'd be on Venus in about fifty hours.

He heard Tod busy down in the other sections of the ship. And a lump came into his throat. The men on Mercury might have more flash to their actions, but Tod was taking a worse chance, and doing it because he was willing to try anything Jerry wanted.

He remembered his idea of letting Dick and Tod down and getting a routine job on a freighter, and it seemed that he must have been another person. Then he gulped. Men were supposed to see their whole life over again before they died—was this some such premonition?

Jerry settled his doubts by swinging the ship about a touch with the steering tubes, and then cutting in the big rocket to even more power. For this run, he'd be using a full two and a quarter gravities. They'd need all the speed they could get as they came near the sun. He considered it again, and changed it to two and a half.

Below, Tod let out a yelp of surprise, but he didn't call up any criticism. He was probably agreeing that they could stand the threat of blowing the tubes better than the risk of not getting to the sun and away fast enough.

Something sounded from the front, and Jerry looked up in surprise. A sheet of shining metal was being slid against the big quartz port on the outside hull. Tod must have gone out between the hulls. Jerry tapped on the glass.

The engineer's head came up in a space helmet. The helmet touched the quartz, and Jerry could just make out the inquiry. He leaned forward and shouted. "Where'd you get them?"

Tod followed his pointing finger, glancing at the metal sections. "Emergency repair for the ports . . . lighter than more quartz. I just sort of polished them up."

The helmet popped down, and more sections came into place, to fit between the hull against both the inner and outer quartz panels. The view of the blazing sun disappeared. From now on, all navigation would have to be done by means of the tele-panels, as was done on some of the newer freighters.

For a while it felt strange, but then it was a relief not to be able to see the they were approaching.

Cautiously, he began setting the ship into a spin along its axis. It required tricky work, and combinations of the steering tubes he hadn't tried before. Most of the energy seemed to be wasted in setting up side-sways that had to be corrected.

Tod watched silently when he came in with his work finished. "Be a blamed sight harder to snap out of this than to get into it, too," he warned.

Jerry had been worrying about the same thing. But that was another of the problems he'd have to solve after they got away from the sun, if they did get away.

The sun in the panels seemed larger than ever, whenever Jerry glanced at it. He knew that it was an illusion; his imagination was only playing tricks on him. But he couldn't shake it off. Tod seemed to share his fascination.

"Sure kicking up a commotion down there," he observed, pointing to a long tongue of flame that had seemed to leap out thousands of miles from the sun's surface. "Wonder if he knows we're coming?"

It already seemed warmer, too. Jerry finished one bit of correcting for a bad attempt, then glanced at the thermometer. It registered an even seventy-two degrees, as it should. It felt like ninety. Maybe the humidity control was off? He checked the gauge on that, but found it was where it belonged.

"I guess we'll stop imagining when the real thing starts," he observed.

Tod nodded soberly.

Bit by bit, the ship began to spin. They wouldn't need any rapid rate of turn—once around every five minutes was all Jerry wanted. It wouldn't give them enough rotary speed to throw them sideways toward the outer walls. There'd been talk once in the old days of spinning ships for that purpose—to give them a feeling of weight, and let them walk along the outer walls. That was when ships had blasted up at high acceleration for a few minutes and coasted long months the rest of the way without power, in weightless flight. If it had ever been used, it must have required a terrific rate of spin. He wondered how they'd solved the problem of navigating. Perhaps handling a ship in spin was one of the lost arts.

Finally, Jerry timed it by the tele-panels, and found that it was close enough. There was no apparent error; he couldn't detect anything wrong with the course as a result of his fooling with the steering rockets. Now all they had to do was wait.

Tod brought up the supper and sat down beside Jerry to stare at the spinning image of the sun in the tele-panels.

"It's not too late to back out now, Tod," Jerry told him.

The old man shook his head. "I've seen almost everything else, kid; I'm gonna see this through. And if that mayor thinks he'll have a yarn to spin, he should hear what I'll be saying if we get out of this alive!"

He chewed on, hardly watching his plate as he ate.

The sun was a magnet that drew their eyes. Now it was a trifle larger in the panels.

Jerry stood up finally. "Okay, Tod. I gave you your chance. Now I'm ordering you to hit the sack. When we wake up, it will be too late to turn back, and we'll have to get used to the idea. We'll go crazy sitting here!"

"Don't have far to go," Tod said, and he managed a chuckle. His voice was suddenly approving. "You're all right, Captain. You're getting sense, even if you are a fool. Hitting the sack till we can't change our minds is the best idea you've come up with. Only, Jerry, you get your clothes off this time and wash them out before you turn in. We've still got the water, and you're gonna use it!"

Jerry smiled slowly, and put his arm over the old man's shoulder. Tod bristled for a second, and then he chuckled again. For a moment, there were glints in his eyes that might have been tears.

"Darned near raised you, lad. Never had any other kids of my own. And dadgum it, I ain't sorry now!"

He stomped off to his hammock before Jerry could answer, snorting to himself.

Jerry turned to his own hammock quickly, with a lump in his throat. But it felt good, somehow. It cut through his worries and made him feel that all the trouble and danger out there was worthwhile, even if they didn't live through it.

CHAPTER 14/

Solar Barbecue

HEAT woke Jerry up. He lay on the hammock with only a thin cover over him, but he was sweating. He put out his hand to turn the cabin thermometer down, and found that the walls were warmer than the air.

Then it came back to him, and he sat up with a jerk. It was too late to turn back, all right. They must be well on their way toward their near meeting with the sun.

Tod was still sleeping, though, and Jerry was careful not to awaken him. He slipped into the galley, conscious of the warmth of the deck under his feet. From the little freezer, he took cold juice. The idea of coffee didn't appeal to him, as a rule, and it was impossible this morning. He shook his head at the idea. He heated one of the canned waffles, buttered it, and dug out strips of crisp bacon from another heated can.

The control room was changed. Where the panels had shown a circle of the sun against the black of space, they now showed only sections of the great star, with no space on the panel it occupied, and great leaping flames on the adjacent panels.

He found the air-conditioning control, and set it farther up. The cooling of the ship depended on a simple heat pump that sent jets of hot air into a little turbine that cooled it and turned the heat into electricity, while cool air was circulated through the ship. Its cooling action would continue, no matter how hot the air, up to its maximum level. But it wouldn't do much good to cool air at four hundred degrees down to three hundred, Jerry guessed. It would still be too hot.

The air began cooling off a little, with the device working at full power. Without it, it would have already been unbearably hot. From now on, the heat would rise rapidly as they rushed forward, and it would cool off much more slowly.

The terrific radiation of the sun could force the heat in. But space was a vacuum, one of the best possible insulators, and it would take a long time for the ship to lose whatever heat it picked up. It was one of the little things he had overlooked the day before.

At the moment, the feeling that they could no longer change course had made Jerry almost indifferent to the danger. He felt lazy and indolent, without the pressure of responsibility weighing on him, and he nursed the feeling, knowing that the less he exerted himself or tensed up the better he would last later.

He went down to his little cabin and dressed in the wrinkled but clean uniform that no longer showed any signs of ever having come from Space Institute. There they had been expected to be spotless, without a wrinkle. He wondered how well they'd enforce such a rule on a racing ship.

Tod was still sleeping. The air had actually cooled down a little as the heat pump labored to move the warmth into the ship batteries in the form of electricity. It would rise soon enough.

He went back to his breakfast, drawing the last taste of pleasure out of it. Tod came in and joined him, just as he was taking the last mouthful. The old man had automatically used the other half of the cans he had opened. He nodded self-consciously, as if ashamed of his weakness the night before.

Now the thermometer fascinated them more than the panels that showed the sun. It had dropped for a few minutes, but now it was rising again. The air was as warm as it had been when Jerry first awoke, and it seemed to be creeping up steadily.

He snapped out of his mood of relaxation, and began trying to compare the actual temperature with what he had expected at this distance. The pyrometers indicated that the hull was still within the figures he had guessed at, but the air was warming more than he had expected. It was over ninety now, and going up.

The thrust of two and a half times Earth weight against them added to their discomfort, too.

Tod reached out for the wall thermometer, and scowled at it. "One hundred," he announced. He went down the shaft, and came back with the suits. "We might as well put these on now—no sense getting all steamed up until we have to."

Jerry climbed into his with more fondness for the suit than he had ever expected to feel. He pulled down the helmet, and then glanced at the air tanks in surprise. Tod had coupled on an extra one, ready to switch over when the first ran short. They were good for six hours each, and one should have been more than enough. But he let it go.

Inside, the temperature seemed to be normal again.

The panels showed the sun now as a great mottled plain of fire. The spots stood out on it strongly, and every detail of the leaping prominences that sprang up from it were revealed. These were long tongues of thin gases that sometimes went up for a hundred thousand miles from the surface.

It might have been small, as stars go, but the 864,000 mile-diameter globe still made even Jupiter seem totally insignificant. Its pull was enough to reach out through billions of miles and hold Pluto in an orbit, unable to escape.

The thermometer on the wall stood at the top of the

column now; it was probably considerably more than the hundred and forty degrees it indicated.

Tod shook his head suddenly, and went down toward the engine room. Jerry heard the muffled sounds of his activity through his helmet, and glanced down to see the old man dragging the whole heat pump outfit into the central shaft. He struggled with it, not quite able to lift it against the thrust of the rocket.

Jerry slid down to help. Together, they could just get it into the shaft. Then Tod hit a lever on the wall of the shaft, and the bottom cover swung shut, sealing the shaft off from the engine room. He set the heat pump on the shaft cover and adjusted it carefully. Then he went up the shaft, closing all the seals, until the whole tube was sealed off from the rest of the ship, except for the control room and the galley. He brought a tank of water out from the galley, and then closed that. Finally, he sealed off the control room.

"All the controls I need to fight the heat are here," he said, pointing to the bottom of the shaft. "I figure we can cool off this little tube better'n we can the whole ship."

Jerry wondered how he'd get to the controls. Then he realized there was nothing he could do, even if he were there. The ship would have to care for itself. There was nothing more they could do. But he felt lost without any idea of what was going on.

His wrist watch ticked on, sounding loud and slow in the space suit. Fifteen minutes later, Tod dropped water onto the cover of the shaft which was now their deck. It began to dry almost at once. The next time, it boiled. The walls of the shaft had reached over two hundred degrees, in spite of the laboring of the air-cooling heat pump.

The suits were still taking it. He wondered whether the ship was doing as well.

They must be getting close to their nearest approach—perihelion. The temperature seemed to jump upward with each second. Now the water in the tank began boiling by itself. Tod frowned, and held it so that most of the steam went through one of the smaller openings off the shaft. Heat waves danced in. He threw the water out and closed the lid quickly.

Jerry couldn't take any more of it. He began scrambling up toward the control room. He had to have some idea of how the ship was taking it, of the time, and of how close they were.

The control room was a blaze of heat—hot enough so that it seemed to strike through his helmet as he threw the door open, dashed in, and closed it after him. He took one look at the clock, and another at the sun. They weren't yet at perihelion, though they were getting close. But the hull temperature was higher than it should have been.

He jerked back into the cooler shaft—if cool in any degree could be applied to it—and snapped the control room door behind him. His brief exposure had taxed the cooling ability of his suit to the limit, and he found himself sweating inside it.

He slumped down beside Tod, trying to figure the time by counting the pulse he could feel in his throat. It should be seventy a minute, but he decided to consider it eighty, to make up for the added strain. It didn't work too well, though; he kept getting the ticking of his watch mixed up with it.

For a moment he considered yanking his suit off, grabbing the watch, and closing the suit again. But he wouldn't be able to do it fast enough.

The little turbine on the heat pump was turning furiously, but it was losing the battle. Tod moved over toward the water, fuel and oxygen controls he had installed—long wires that led through tiny holes in the shaft. He pulled them back, starting with the water.

It may have made a difference in the ship as a whole, but the heat still seemed to go on rising in the shaft. Now sweat was running down Jerry's face, and he was beginning to gasp for breath. Tod's face was turning red, behind the helmet, and his breathing was also coming faster.

Jerry decided that fifteen minutes must have passed. He forced himself up and began climbing to the control room again. Tod's eyes were reproachful. But the heat that leaked into the tube couldn't be helped; it had to be done.

Jerry paused at the door, dreading what must be done. He gritted his teeth, forced the door open, and slipped through. The control room was a furnace. A piece of paper he touched crumbled under his fingers, dried and brittle in the heat. The clock showed that only eight minutes had passed, but the hull was still rising in temperature. It couldn't stand much more.

He reeled against the padded seat, trying to force his mind off his suffering body. The sun wasn't a mere point that could be passed suddenly; it was like a wall almost nine feet wide as seen from a distance of fifty feet. The ship was just creeping across the surface of it, at a distance of five million miles.

Turning the hull faster would do no good, even if he could manipulate it; it simply couldn't radiate the heat as fast as it was being poured in. He blinked the streams of sweat out of his eyes, sipping at the water tube in his suit. If he could reduce the area, or find a better surface . . .

The idea crept in slowly, while his mind spun in the heat. Then it was hard to concentrate. The room kept going around in circles! He caught himself, realizing that the ship was spinning.

He forced his hands to the control board and cut off the thrust of the rocket. Even that little source of heat would have to be stopped. Then he reached the steering controls and hit it. He waited until the ship was turned so that the next steering rocket pointed the same way, and touched that.

The *Last Hope* heeled over slowly, turning her tail

toward the sun. He began delicately touching the steering tubes now to stop the turn.

He couldn't be sure that it was perfect—the spin of the ship and the agony of breathing made good control almost impossible. But it seemed to be steady.

There was nothing else he could do. He forced his way to the door, swaying at each step. The door seemed to resist his efforts, but it came open, and he got through it somehow. He even managed to close it.

There was no feeling of weight now. The big rocket was off, and they were drifting on at the speed they had built up. It would have to be sufficient.

He pushed himself down the shaft, floating to a landing beside Tod. The old man seemed to be in worse condition than he was, in spite of the time he'd spent in the control room, but one bushy eyebrow lifted weakly.

Jerry lay gasping, slowly getting some control of himself. The shaft was cooler, at least, than the rest of the ship, and the refrigerating unit in his suit began to work better. He leaned over and quickly explained what he had done.

Tod nodded weakly. "Good idea. Should have thought of it. Rear end's mostly rocket tube—and that'll take the heat."

It was also thicker, Jerry knew and it could hold back more of the solar radiation. The lining of the tube was meant to stand nearly impossible temperature.

They must be drawing away, he thought. The sun would try to hold them, but their speed would carry them on. Yet it would be too long before the ship could get far enough away for the heat to radiate away faster than it was being shoved at them by the sun.

The air in his suit seemed damp and sticky. He realized he was sweating faster than the water-removal unit could work.

His mind wandered. He began to think of all the cool breezes he had known, and then of the frozen surface of

Europa, white with its covering of frozen air and deep-buried ice. He shouldn't have left it.

Daniel had gone into the fiery furnace. There were fakirs on Earth who still claimed they could walk across a bed of hot coals. The surface temperature of the sun is six thousand degrees Kelvin—a lot more than that Fahrenheit.

He swallowed a salt tablet from the little holder and took another drink from the tube near his lips. The water was hot, sickening. But it helped.

He leaned over and touched his helmet to Tod's. "Tod! Tod!"

The old man looked up slowly, reason coming back into his eyes. "Eh?"

"What about the fuel—will it stand this temperature?"

Tod made an effort to snap out of the semi-trance he was in. He puckered his face into a knot of concentration.

"Won't explode," he decided. "But it might boil over—I don't think it will, but it might. Then, if it hits a bit of tin or solder . . ."

He shuddered, and slipped back into the pain and the dullness Jerry was fighting against. It was physical agony to breath now. His suit felt like fire against his skin. He got to his feet carefully and pulled himself up the shaft a few feet. There he carefully balanced himself out away from everything and let go.

By squirming about he could manage to avoid contact with most of the suit. But nothing could help the thick heat of the air that seared his lungs and seemed to suck all the moisture from his throat and nostrils.

It couldn't get worse. But it continued to grow hotter. The suit couldn't begin to handle the extreme temperature now. Jerry moaned with each breath that sent his chest out against the hot fabric and plastic. But he had to breathe in short, gasping gulps at an ever quickening pace.

He knew that he was reaching his limit. Tod had already passed out, which was a blessing to the old man. Here was one of the places where youth had the advantages of endurance, but he knew it was a mixed blessing.

He knew he would soon faint. He looked down at the valve on his bottle of air and saw that it was half-empty. With weak hands, he replaced it with the full one beside it. The effort brought him up against the shaft wall and forced his shoulder to touch the hot suit again. He screamed, but it pulled him together for a moment.

With his last bit of energy, he forced himself down beside Tod, and began the agonizing job of changing air bottles. There was no way of knowing how long they would remain unconscious, if they survived. He'd begun to doubt that there was much chance of that, but he had to be sure they wouldn't die by suffocating in their suits when the air ran out.

He lifted Tod up into the air, pulled the suit away from the old body, and held it steady until he could be sure no motion would throw it against a wall. Then he again pulled himself up to his former position and worked his clothing away from his body.

The ship was swimming faster now—turning around and around. Each breath was a surge of fire into his lungs. His eyes filled with red spots, while every cell of his body was crying in anguish. Slowly, the red spots went away.

The ship drifted on past the sun, and he drifted into unconsciousness that was still filled with flaming agony.

CHAPTER 15 /

Venus Calling Mars!

HEAT was still radiating from the walls, and the air in the suit was stifling when Jerry revived. He saw by the valve on his tank that it was half-full, which meant that he had been unconscious for about three hours—probably less, since the rate of breathing had been faster.

His entire back must have touched against a wall, because it was burning worse than all the sunburns in the universe. Sunburn! It was exactly that—sunburn in a place where walls of metal gave no real shade!

But he knew that the heat was falling at last, since he would never have revived otherwise. It meant that they were still in a ship that was capable of functioning. It had been a close call, but they'd gotten through.

He groaned as he reached for the shaft, clenched his teeth, and began climbing up in the weightlessness that still existed. He could never have made it against gravity. When he got the door open, he found that there was little difference between the shaft and the control room now; the room was in the shadow of the ship's tail, and the walls were beginning to lose heat.

He left the door open, and studied his position as best he could in the tele-panels. There was no way of being sure of how he stood, however, while the ship continued to spin. He began the difficult job of trying to pull it out.

Either he was lucky, or he had learned while getting it into the spin. It took less than ten minutes to bring it to a fixed position. Now he could find where they were.

He stopped to swallow another salt tablet, a mixed vitamin pill of heroic proportions, and a few of the chocolate tablets that could be brought to his mouth by turning his head. The water was tepid, but he drank a little. There was nothing he could do about the nausea and headache, or the feeling of a raging fever. They'd have to wait until the ship could cool further.

His position agreed with what it should, according to the clock, and he didn't bother to check it again. Minor corrections could be made later. Venus was in line, and he could set down there comfortably by using slightly less than two gees of deceleration.

He steered the ship around until its tail pointed toward the planet and adjusted the controls before cutting on the big rocket. The weight was less then he'd been used to for days now, but it seemed to crush him. He was so weak that he could barely stand against it.

Two hours later, the control room was cool enough for him to remove his suit. Hastily he applied unguents to his back and went down to bring Tod up. The old man was still unconscious, but breathing normally.

Jerry stripped him and covered his inflamed body with the unguent. It contained one of the Martian plant drugs, and usually could produce healing of a normal burn in a few hours. The cabins were still too hot, but the air flowing in was cooling them rapidly. Jerry waited a few minutes, and then put Tod on a hammock and crawled into another. He swallowed a drug that would kill the remaining pain and make him sleep.

Tod woke him. The old man had recovered remarkably during the few hours. He looked smaller and more shriveled, but he seemed to be in almost his normal condition.

Jerry took a long breath of the cool, sweet air, let it out reluctantly, and began dressing. The burns were almost entirely gone, and most of his other symptoms were going. Tod waited for him to go up to the control room and then went into the galley to collect plates of food.

"Bust cans all over. Galley looks like pigs lived in it. Whole ship's a mess. I've scraped up some of it. You'll have to eat toasted cheese and double-baked crackers. Everything else is ruined," Tod told him.

Jerry took the food gratefully. The cheese seemed to have gone through odd changes in its can, but it was edible. He downed a glass of water first. They still had enough of that to last, at least. The condenser had drawn it out of the air as it cooled.

He saw that the metal shields over the ports had been removed, and realized that Tod had been busy for hours already.

"Getting old," the engineer muttered. "Can't take it. Sorry I conked out on you, kid."

"Sorry I put you through it," Jerry answered.

They finished the food and went down, to begin cleaning up the mess in the ship. They couldn't do anything about the paint that was gone, or the supplies that were ruined, except to pile the junk into one of the storage rooms, out of the way. But they felt better as the *Last Hope* began to look like a space ship again.

They landed on Venus at seven A.M., Tuesday, the twenty-fourth. In spite of all the troubles, they were two hours closer to Dick's schedule than they had been when they left Ganymede. But they were still over a hundred hours behind, and there was very little chance to make it up now.

Jerry expected no trouble from the pleasant, friendly people of Venus, and he was right. They were too polite to ask questions about the condition of his ship, but they pitched in quietly and began restocking it with smooth efficiency.

Venus was unlike any of the other inhabited worlds. Here the domes were used to protect the inhabitants from the atmosphere, instead of to keep air in. The world was only slightly smaller than Earth, and its atmosphere was a trifle deeper. Here, near the pole, it was warm, but not too hot—the dense clouds that covered the planet reflected enough heat to prevent the temperature rising too far, and the eighty-hour day was still short enough to keep a balance between the cold of its shadowy night and the heat of the day that was not too unpleasant.

The big trouble had been with the air. There was some oxygen and too much carbon dioxide, but only a few traces of water. The dense clouds had actually been thin upper veils, appearing so dense only because the violent winds and churning atmoshphere had kept them in violent motion and completely spread out. On the ground, those same winds had whipped the surface into a dust bowl, and eroding, stinging hurricanes of dust-filled air were constantly blowing.

But now the air was improving. The water and oxygen had apparently once been common, but a strange life-form of a weird crystalline nature not completely understood had managed to trap most of them. Men had found that the desert plants from Earth could be grown on the harsh, dry soil, and the plants had flourished far beyond the pioneer dreams. They were rapidly breaking the carbon dioxide down to oxygen. They also proved capable of breaking up the crystalline forms, and liberating the oxygen and water in them. Biologists had determined that it was a soil bacterium brought with the plants that did that, but it didn't matter. In another hundred years, Venus had hopes of having an atmosphere as wholesome as that of Earth. Even now, it could be breathed for short times, with the help of a little extra oxygen.

The pioneers had flourished here, and grown pleasantly soft, something like the Spaniards of old California. Their houses, under the domes, were gems of form and color, and their soft voices were a welcome contrast to the buzz and rasp of the rest of the system.

Jerry found the Commission office open, and presented his papers. The agent looked up at him, smiling. "You've had a difficult time, young man. I can see that. It's a pity that you can't win. We were hoping you would, when our ship was wrecked among the asteroids."

"You mean Mars is sure of winning?" Jerry asked sharply.

The official bowed slightly. "Through no fault of yours. I believe you would still have an excellent chance, if it weren't for that unfortunate ruling. Mars, of course, brought it to the attention of the Commission."

"What ruling?"

The man frowned slightly.

"I'm so sorry—I thought you would have heard. The ruling states that all the men on board a racing ship at the beginning of a race must be present on the same ship at the end of that race. Unfortunately, of course, your brother is on Mars!"

He held out one of the thick books of rules which no pilot could hope to know in full, pointing out the section. Jerry read it over quickly, and turned to the index. He ran down several cross references quickly, before handing it back.

"So that's why the Martians were so willing to take care of Dick!" he said bitterly.

The official shook his head gently. "No, give them credit where it is due. They are as humane as you or we. They have fought a tremendous fight against a difficult world and have succeeded beyond what anyone could believe; now they continue to fight equally hard, and with equally little sense of anything but victory, even though they have won their planet. But they do not offer their hospitality in their hospitals for anything but mercy. It's a pity so much of the old hostility between you and them still exists."

It was all very pretty, but it had nothing to do with the race. Jerry went back to an earlier statement. "You say you think we could still win—does that mean that Mars isn't much ahead of us in time?"

"A few hours, I believe. We have only the rough returns on their course, but I believe I can say you would stand some chance if your brother were still with you." The agent's face was filled with genuine regret.

Dick was on Mars, though—and Mars was a long way away. There wouldn't be time to pick him up and get back to Earth. Jerry checked back over his ideas. He wanted no repetition of his foolishness on Ganymede.

"The rule doesn't say that all the men have to be on the ship during the whole race, does it?" he asked, to be sure.

The official shot him a sharp glance, and picked up the book, thumbing through it quickly. He smiled slightly, and then frowned. "No—apparently it was overlooked in revising the book this time. Or perhaps it was intended that a sick man could be dropped at a suitable planet and picked up later. That is entirely possible. You're quite correct—if you could remove your brother from Mars to your ship and still reach Earth before the ship from Mars, you would be the winner—unless, of course, there is another ship in the lead that I know nothing about."

Jerry sat down, reaching for the star maps that lay on one of the desks. The official went to a closet and came back carrying a calculator similar to the one with which the boy was familiar, and another more elaborate machine. Jerry took the simple one with a brief word of thanks.

He checked his distances and locations of the planets,

and began feeding in the information. It would mean a long trip, and he was sure it wouldn't work. But he had to depend on facts, and not on his own beliefs.

He stared at the figures that came out. It would take over sixty hours to Mars, and at least four there for fuel and to pick up Dick. Then Mars was farther from Earth now than at the start of the race. Another fifty-two hours. At the very least, a hundred and sixteen hours, instead of the forty-eight hours that would be required to reach Earth directly from Venus. That was a difference of nearly three days!

"It won't work, of course," the official said regretfully. "I'd considered it myself, though I didn't have the exact thrust you felt it was safe to use."

Jerry looked at the figures, trying to find something wrong, but he knew they were right. He seized on another idea. "But I was a replacement for Dick—I took his place as pilot. The *Last Hope* operates with only two men aboard normally."

"Not a chance," the agent told him firmly, though still in a gentle tone of voice. "Your brother served as part of the crew to Mars, and then took off for Jupiter, before you put back. The plea wouldn't work."

Jerry hadn't counted on it. He'd known how weak it was when he mentioned the idea, but it had given him time to think. "Does it matter how Dick gets off Mars, provided he's on the *Last Hope* when we land on Earth?"

"There's nothing in the rules which says you can't move him by black magic, even, if you like," the man answered. Then his face took on a startled expression.

There was nothing lazy about him as he jumped back to his desk and reached for an elaborate radio set there. "Give me through to interplanet, on top priority, and then seal the beam to me," he ordered.

A few seconds later the set buzzed. "They're relaying directly from here," he explained, as he picked up the microphone again. "Venus calling Mars! Venus calling Mars! Venus calling Mars!"

He dropped the receiver, and they waited while the waves traveled out at 186,000 miles a second across the long distance to Mars. The answer took still more time to come back.

"Mars acknowledging. Go ahead, Venus!"

"Give me a list of all ships which will leave Eros within the next twenty-four hours, and particularly of all ships of Earth registry, together with their normal operating times for the trip to Earth or to Venus!"

Again the wait was a long one, while Jerry hung over the edge of the desk. On the major planets, the representative of the Commission was obviously a person who could work miracles.

The official smiled at him. "I'm not being partial, young man. As an accredited racer, you have the right to appeal to me for all the help you wish, so long as it does not operate to the exclusion of the rights of others, or does not violate any rule in that book. I suspect you haven't been making the fullest use of that right, but it's a pleasure to be of help to you."

The list began coming in eventually. Only one Earth ship was leaving—the *Chicago Queen,* with a listed acceleration to halfway of slightly over one gravity. The official asked and got a connection to her skipper, Captain Miles, and turned the microphone over to Jerry.

Miles was more than agreeable to help. "Get your brother to come on board, and I'll take off in half an hour after he's here. I haven't posted my departure yet. And Blaine, don't try to meet me at halfway; I'm too slow. Figure out the best meeting place, and I'll go there, even if it is out of my way. I've been waiting for almost thirty years to see an Earth ship give Mars a good run for its money, and I don't care how much trouble it is."

Jerry went back to his calculator. It turned out that Miles would help most if he set a course almost exactly between Earth and Venus. That way, they could rendezvous in approximately forty-eight hours, and Jerry should be able to go on to Earth in another thirty-two hours or so, for a total time of eighty hours. It wasn't all he could have wanted, but it would have to do.

Captain Miles got off the channel, and Jerry began trying to reach Dick. There was some difficulty, since he was supposed to be out in the recreation section, but they finally brought him to the radio.

"Hi, Jerry," he called. "I hear you've been having bad luck. Forget it. We can't cry over spilled milk. And I'm feeling fine. How much is this costing you, anyhow?"

Jerry grinned at his brother's voice. "Don't ask foolish questions, Dick. Get out of that hospital and check in on the *Chicago Queen* as fast as you can. I've got to pick you up if all the rules are to be met. And if you have any trouble, they tell me the local office of the Commission will see that you get help. Get going!"

He hung up, without wasting more time, and turned back to thank the man who had made even this slim chance possible. But the agent shrugged it off.

"As I told you, I would do the same for Mars—it's my duty. Unofficially, however, I wish you a great deal of luck. I don't think you can make it, but I'll hope that you do. Now you'd better get back to your ship."

He was still going to lose more than a day, of course—but somehow he felt better about it. As long as there was even a slim chance, he had something to fight for.

He didn't even stop to buckle on his helmet as he ran out toward the official car that was waiting for him.

CHAPTER 16 /

Needle in a Spacestack

THEY were still refueling the ship and loading supplies when Jerry reached the field. This time, the work was being done by efficient machines, instead of by manual labor—with the result that it was actually going slower on such a small ship as the *Last Hope*. Tod was checking off the lists, while men were busy painting the ship ang getting rid of the debris and damage caused by the heat of the sun.

The story of the solar crisping had apparently been spread, and people were drifting quietly toward the field. Tod talked too much!

Jerry took the manifests and read down the lists of what was already on board. He estimated quickly, and signaled the official in charge of the loading.

"Call your men off as soon as you've got these items on board. I'm taking off as soon as it's done!"

The official looked surprised and doubtful, but he bent forward slightly, smiling courteously. "As you wish, Captain Blaine."

Tod grabbed the lists back, but Jerry shook his head and headed across the field toward the ship, where workmen were collecting their tools and paint, and beginning to stream down the ladder.

"We've got to get off at once, Tod," he told his engineer. "The provisions and fuel I checked off will carry us with a few drops to spare, and we can't wait here forever. I've already spent too much time. Five hours here, when we could have had the whole job done on Io in four!"

He watched the last of the workmen leave, and went up the ladder, with Tod at his heels. Inside, he gave a quick summation of what had happened.

"How come you never showed me the rule book?" he asked, finally.

Tod brought his eyebrows together. "Dick took it with him to the Commission meeting on the Moon. I haven't seen it since. Thought you had it."

"I didn't even know there was one—I've been going on what the newspapers printed. And I've been butting my head against stone walls all along, because I didn't have sense enough to ask for some of the help I could have had." He wasn't too surprised that the book had disappeared. Dick had always had a habit of memorizing nearly everything he read, and paying little attention to books.

Finally, the last of their scanty supplies were on board, and the all-clear signal sounded. Jerry checked the clock—now indicating noon—and cut the blast on. They were lifting through the atmosphere, going cautiously in order to avoid too much friction, until they reached the roiling layer of the thin clouds. The ship was buffeted about in the gales that swept the planet for a moment more, and then Jerry cut on full power, until the needle registered two gees.

It seemed more normal now than the gravity of Venus, which was seven-eighths that of Earth.

This time there was no planet waiting for them, but only a spot in space, listed under X, Y, and Z numbers that had come into use to divide space into small divisions. It was a lot different from heading for a planet, where it was always possible to correct any error as you came into its range.

This time he was meeting a tiny mote in space—a space ship that couldn't weigh more than a few hundred tons, and which the radar screen could locate at no more than a few thousand miles. In addition, he had to make sure that he zeroed his speed at that spot, or there would be hours wasted in juggling back and forth.

He had to worry about the skill of Captain Miles, too, who was probably long out of navigation school, and had gotten used to setting his course by the sight of the planets. Some of the older pilots were capable of stopping dead still on a dime anywhere between Mercury and Jupiter. Others couldn't have found Mars without being able to spot it in their screens.

It was something with which he'd had no personal experience. Just how do you know when you've completely neutralized your speed, out millions of miles from nowhere?

It seemed simple enough, after cutting through Jupiter's gases and shaving the sun. But it was a better test of his real ability than all those stunts had been.

He tried to remember everything that had been in the books about it, and finally gave up. The books hadn't helped him too much, so far. They were part of his knowledge and valuable enough, but they were useful only when coupled in with practical experience. His calculations had been learned in school, but the feeling of the ship had come with practice.

He figured things as carefully as he could, and let it go at that. If he had to jockey back and forth—well, the papers would call him a hot-rocket jockey, and he'd have to live up to it.

He reached turnover point and swept the *Last Hope* around with a single long blast from one of the side tubes, correcting for his swing immediately afterward. She held steady in her decelerating position. Tod grunted.

"What they teach you in school, Tod," he commented. "It saves time and fuel. Only it took a long time for me to find out that it really could be done that way."

Forty-nine hours out from Venus, Jerry cut the blast and went dead. He checked his position carefully, and could detect no sign of drift, and no error. He was at least correct to within a few thousand of a per cent—which was still too big an error, if it existed.

There was no sign of the *Chicago Queen*. He stretched out the range of his screen to the limit and waited. He couldn't have missed that far!

He began sending out a call on the radio. An answer came back almost at once. The *Queen* had had a little trouble getting fast clearance on Mars until the Commission had stepped in. She'd rendezvous in ten minutes.

Jerry waited, leaving his radio on to give them a homing signal. The screen suddenly lighted up and began beeping at him. The *Queen* was crawling up, going just a trifle too fast, and a bit offside.

Probably they were both slightly in error, but it was close. They would pass within half a mile, and with less than five miles an hour error in matching speeds.

But it wasn't good enough. Jerry began a fast flip-over and prepared to try to match course with the *Queen*. It was hard to maneuver at such close quarters, and he couldn't use more than a touch on the big tube without overshooting. He held it down to low power, and flipped it on quickly, letting go at once. The *Queen* was now drawing near, but more slowly. He began to juggle with the steering tubes, edging toward the spot where they should meet. As she came up almost directly behind, he hit the power again, with a mere flick of his finger that produced a slight jerk.

"Jerry!" It was Dick's voice in the phones. "Hold it there. You're close enough. Captain Miles was worried all the way here that he'd have to go chasing you all over space, like a needle in a haystack. You're a hot pilot, kid—but don't try a perfect match. Most of them are pure fiction out here. I can bridge across. Right, Tod?"

"I reckon so, if you want to be a fool again," the old man said. "I'll have to catch, I suppose."

Jerry stood up, but Dick must have sensed his reaction. "You stay put, Jerry. If something goes wrong, I'll want you at the helm to do your best. Be with you in a second."

He cut off. A few seconds later, the two ships were drifting side by side, a couple hundred feet apart. The difference in their speed was almost unnoticeable.

The air lock of the *Queen* opened, just as an indicator on the control panel told Jerry that Tod must have gone outside. A big figure in a space suit was in the lock.

Dick took a good look across at the *Last Hope*, doubled his legs under him, and jumped. He wasn't even wearing a rope to pull him back! And he hadn't made allowances for the fact that even a big ship will roll a few fractions of an inch when a man jumps from her in space, where nothing holds her anchored firmly.

He was going to miss by several feet, Jerry saw. He came sailing across the space between the ships, a grin on his face. Just as he seemed about to pass over the *Last Hope*, a rope with a weight tied to it sailed up.

Dick caught it easily, and began moving down and out of sight. Tod's toss had been true.

The transshipping was complete. The indicator showed the lock was closing. Jerry heaved a sigh of relief, and acknowledged the call from the *Queen*.

"Glad I could help, Captain Blaine," Miles said. "Too bad you don't have much chance. But give them all you've got."

Jerry thanked him again. But he was getting tired of the universal feeling that he didn't have a chance. He'd never had a chance on this trip, but he was still jockeying the *Last Hope,* and no one had come in for the final landing, according to his knowledge.

He had begun swinging the ship toward Earth the moment Dick was aboard. Now he opened the big rocket tube, and they were on their way home.

A new pip showed up on the screen, traveling at a furious clip! It crossed the screen in seconds and was gone.

Dick was standing in the door of the control room, with one hand outstretched. Now he dropped it and jumped for the screen. "That was a ship—and a racer. No regular liner hits up to that speed!"

"Mars!" Tod muttered from the doorway, behind Dick.

It didn't seem possible. It was an odd route. But there was no question about it.

Jerry reached for the main tube control and then shook his head. He was using all the acceleration he could afford; they'd taken off from Venus with a short supply of fuel. If he pushed it any higher, they'd be stranded somewhere on the way, unable to slow for a landing.

He shook it off, and stood up, sticking out a hand.

"Hi, Dick. You're looking swell."

It was the truth. Dick had never looked better, except for the worried frown over his eyes. It disappeared as he took his brother's hand in a hard grasp. Then a puzzled light came into his eyes.

"You look a lot better than I expected, kid. But I don't know that I like the look on your face. It looks like I'm vacating the position of older brother and fatherly adviser. You're about to tell me to shove over and meet a man my own size, or I miss my guess. How about it, Tod?"

Tod shook his head. "Nope. He's a long ways from your size—and I'm not talking about beef, either. You two go ahead and fight out your own ruckus. I got work to do."

He stuffed a fresh wad of gum into his mouth, and headed down the shaft, leaving them alone. Dick began telling about his stay on Mars, while trying to get all the facts on the race.

Jerry supplied it mechanically. He'd never thought he was as good a man as Dick, but Tod's words had hurt. He'd thought the old man was pleased with the way he'd run the *Last Hope*. It wasn't exactly pleasant to be reminded that he was only a second-rater, even if it was the truth.

It was the first chance he'd really had to talk to Dick, though, since he'd gone to Earth to enter Space Institute, and he tried to make the most of it.

Finally he stood up again, and motioned Dick toward the control panel. "I guess you'll want to get the feel of her?"

Dick sat down, and stood up again quickly. "Nope, I don't, after all. I'm quitting space. Even though we don't win, and Sun Fuels won't back Dad's stuff, I can still get me a job as a fuel engineer there. The representative on Mars told me so."

"But they'll want the fuel, anyhow, won't they?" Jerry hadn't thought of it for days, but it seemed that he'd at least proved that the fuel was all it was supposed to be.

"They're doubtful about it. They think that it's been fuel trouble that's held you up a lot of the time. Even suggested that maybe you had to put back to Mars because of that, and that my eye trouble was a fake. You can't blame them, Jerry. With no real publicity, who'd buy the fuel if they did make it?"

"Then why go back to Earth and take the job?"

Dick shrugged. "Because I've always wanted to be an ordinary engineer—like Dad. Space gets too rich for my blood."

Jerry lay awake for hours, thinking about that. He knew a lot of things he'd never known before. Space was what he wanted, and it wouldn't matter whether he was third assistant wiper on a freighter or captain on the biggest liner out of Earth. He couldn't understand Dick's quitting. One of the things that had been driving him on had been his desire to do what Dick would have done.

Now it seemed that Dick wouldn't have done them. His interest in the race dealt only with the fuel. It made good sense, he supposed, since they would be broke, otherwise; and probably Dick felt that Earth should win as strongly as anyone else.

But that wasn't enough for Jerry, anymore. He felt let down in Dick, and hurt at Tod's lack of respect for him. It was almost as bad as the time Commodore Tenn had called him in to sack him from Space Institute.

He'd just gotten to sleep when Tod came pounding on his shoulder. "Jerry. Hey, Captain!"

"Okay, okay." He rolled out of the hammock, realizing he'd been sleeping in his clothes again. The old man would give him the dickens for that.

But Tod didn't notice. He held out a gummy hand toward the boy. "Fuel! Jerry, the middle tank is leaking—that heat must have weakened an old weld. There isn't a drop left in it, and I can't scrape up more than a gallon that we can salvage!"

Jerry looked at the fuel, and down toward the tracks where more fuel had rubbed off Tod's shoes.

"How much do we have, closest estimate you can make?"

About three hundred gallons, maybe a little less. I measured it at two ninety-six. Dick's down mopping it up, but we can't squeeze anything much out of the mess—it got mixed with everything."

"No tin?"

"Nope. Checked on that. Everything's off the floor."

Jerry leaped up the rail toward the control room and dropped his hands onto the keys of the calculator that had become almost an extension of himself. His eyes checked off the time, and he rechecked position while the calculator digested his figures.

When he finished, Dick and Tod were in the doorway, wiping themselves dry. He threw the figures down on the table, and reached for the main tube control, cutting the acceleration down a notch. Then he swung back.

"We're short. We can't make Earth, unless we want to slow down too far. Our best bet is to set down on Luna Center port and pick up more fuel. We're in luck—the Moon will be right between us and Earth. We haven't got enough left to fight down through an atmosphere, taking it easy all the way, but we can land at Luna Center, I think, without much loss of time."

He handed the paper to them. "I figure we lose about two hours this way, but if I slow down enough, or drift part way, to coddle the fuel, we'll lose more time. Okay, Dick?"

"You're the captain," the other told him. "Seems more sensible to drift a little, but I guess atmospheric landing would eat up a lot of fuel. Okay, kid."

He didn't wait for more, but went on down to his bunk. Tod came over.

"Quit kidding," he told Jerry, and his fingers were making a paper ball out of the calculations. "You mean if we can't make it to Luna, you can correct enough to shoot on by and yell for a tug. And if we get messed up with any more atmospheres and then find we can't, we go down! And we don't walk away."

Jerry nodded. It wouldn't take much to recover if the fuel ran short at Luna Center—the steering tubes held enough reserve for that.

"Yeah," Tod grumbled. "Sure. But I wonder what you'd of done if Dick wasn't here?"

He left it at that, and Jerry couldn't make any sense of it.

"After all," the boy pointed out, "this is Dick's ship. And he won't make much good as an engineer if he winds up in pieces. As captain, I'm responsible for the crew, Tod."

Tod nodded glumly. "Yep. We've got to consider a lot of things now. Well, you're the captain."

CHAPTER 17/

Lunar Landing

IT WAS going to be ticklish, Jerry knew. He had Tod over the main fuel tank where all the remaining amount was, ready to yell the moment he saw bottom. That would leave about four gallons in the pipe, and should be enough to sheer off and go into a long elliptical orbit around the Moon.

He came down cautiously, trying not to waste a drop of the precious stuff. There was no opportunity to dance about while making sure the ground under him was just where it should be.

Waiting for the cry from Tod became a nerve-wracking thing. Then it was too late, and he knew he had to land. He eased down steadily, seeing the landing dome open under him in the tele-screen. He'd radioed ahead, and they'd agreed to have their fuel ready, with plenty of men to load it in. But now he didn't have any real hope of winning. That had all washed out, some-where hours ago.

The blast struck ground, and he cut it down. A sud-den yell from Tod came up, just as they touched, with-out a sign of roughness. The fuel had lasted better then he had expected.

"Whole bottom's clean," Tod reported. "Didn't want

to worry you till I felt us down. Just made it. Dad-burned pretty landing, kid."

Dick echoed it. "The best landing I've seen in the *Last Hope* since I've owned her."

Jerry grinned at them, but it was purely mechanical. He was too sick at the almost certain defeat they were facing. They might have passed the other rocket on the way in—at the end of a long run, the racers frequently had to hold down their acceleration because the tubes were heating too much. And there was no way of judging speed accurately on a screen, without a longer study than he had made of it.

But by the time they could load and get to Earth, the other ship could practically coast in.

He saw men coming onto the field, and knew that there was air in the landing dome again. He slipped from his seat and started to leave, just as an erratic buzz sounded from the radio. It wasn't a call for him, obviously; it must be a side-band effect from some other radio not properly tuned.

But he picked up the phones and listened in. He could barely make it out, even when he adjusted the tuning. ". . . Coming in, approximately three hours. Clear landing field, Earth . . .!"

"The winning ship," Tod guessed, and Jerry nodded. They really were working a sloppy signal, since their beam to Earth was spilling over, instead of being tight.

Then he saw the men below looking up, and raised his head. Barely over the surface of the Moon, but heading on to Earth, a streak shot by, leaving a trail of flame dying in the sky. It was the greenish-blue of Io, though, and not that of Mars.

Jerry tried to grin. At least Mars wouldn't win—unless they had already landed! But it didn't really matter any more. He had thought he'd already given up hope, but now he knew what losing really felt like.

"I guess we might as well go down and concede. No

use rushing to get to Earth now," Dick said. "Too bad, Jerry. You pretty near did the impossible, anyhow."

Jerry faced him, conscious that his lips seemed too stiff to move, and that his voice was all wrong. But it had to be said. "I'm still captain, Dick. We won't quit until we reach Earth—and we'll make the best time we can, too. I don't care if we are the last ones in, now—but we're not quitting."

He turned on his heel and headed out through the top air lock. The little ladder seemed to sway in his hands, though he knew it couldn't. He saw the drums of fuel waiting on the ground, and jumped the final ten feet to land easily under the one sixth pull of the Moon.

"We won't need all of that," he told the port official. "Just get me ten of those drums into the tanks, and do it as fast as you can. I'm a little overdue."

He tried to smile at that, but it was probably a sorry attempt. The official didn't seem to notice, though. He pointed to ten of the drums, and men sprang to lift them up the ramp that was being pushed up against the fueling ports of the ship.

"One at a time," the official warned them. "Make it fast, but make it smooth for Captain Blaine."

There was more enthusiasm in the answering cries than Jerry had expected. He watched the men moving along efficiently, glad that there were none of the Venus mechanical gadgets around to slow things up. Earth used machines, but they worked!

The official stood beside Jerry. "A great race, Captain. Too bad you ran short of fuel."

"Too bad a lot of things, I suppose," Jerry admitted. "But she's a great ship, even if she's only an old mining hot-rocket job, instead of a racer. And the fuel's a miracle. A shame to let them go to waste, isn't it?"

The other frowned. "I don't see them going to waste yet. We're all pretty proud of the way you've handled yourself in this, Captain Blaine. It's been pretty dirty, but I haven't seen even a Martian paper that has anything against you."

Jerry shrugged, and dropped it. Earth was a nice sportsmanlike loser. Mars was the big businessman type that got things done. They'd praise him—but they'd go right on taking the business away from Earth, and their success would simply make the next race dirtier. It didn't have to be—the race could have been one of the finest things in the Solar System.

"Mars got in when?" he asked.

"Huh? She hasn't landed yet—we're expecting her signal any minute, but she's still cutting space from Mercury!"

That was some help. Io probably hadn't hesitated to pull a few tricks, if Jerry knew the miners, but they'd have been a lot cleaner than Mars in their methods.

"Io won't get much business out of winning around the inner planets," he said. "But the miners and freighters there treated me to their best. I'm glad they've got the Classic."

For a second, the official's mouth seemed about to snap off at the jaw socket, from the way his lower jaw fell. Then he caught Jerry's shoulder. "Are you serious? Yeah, you are. Blaine, that rocket from Io isn't even in the match any more! They got into trouble with a tiny meteorite on the way to Venus, and now they're hobbling into Earth's repair docks. You're the first one to get in! The first! Why do you think we got this fuel out to you in such a short time, and without any real notice?"

Jerry's own jaw was dropping, and he saw Tod stopped halfway down the ladder, with his Venus gum cud sticking out of his cheek, motionless.

A messenger came screaming up on a scooter before Jerry could find anything to say. He tossed the official a slip of paper and roared back.

The official took one look at it, and handed it to Jerry.

"Mars just called Earth. They're coming in, expect to land at 11:15 P.M."

"Get that stuff loaded, and put some snap into it!" the official yelled at the men doing the loading. "Mars is coming in—set to land in about two hours. We gotta get this man out of here!"

But the last drum was already being emptied.

The official caught Jerry in two husky arms and tossed him toward the ladder. Jerry's hands came out automatically, and he was scrambling up the little rungs toward the control room. Below him, the ramp was being hastily run back, and men were charging across the field to have it cleared for evacuation of the air.

The all-clear signal came down just as the last man reached safety. They weren't even waiting for evacuation. The dome popped open, and the air went exploding outward, carrying dust from the field with it. Air was precious here, but this was an occasion when air didn't count!

Jerry was in the seat before Tod could swing the air lock shut, and his hands were ready when the indicator showed they were sealed. The *Last Hope* came up from the Moon with a rush, lifting with everything he could cram into her. Right now was no time to worry about the tube, or heat. He was out to beat a time he didn't think could be beat—but it was no longer a matter of a hundred hours. It would be settled in split minutes at the end, where it was up to his skill and the fuel that was driving them on.

He set up his figures quickly, while kicking them into a true course with the foot controls of the steering tubes. There was no time to plan first, and then aim. He had to get there, or as near as he could. And it was hard to miss Earth from here.

Mars was already slowing, but she'd pass him on the way in. He had to get up speed first, and then begin slowing down for the landing. He'd made it in two and a half hours coming out. It was now 9:00 P.M. on the clock—Friday the twenty-seventh, by Earth time. Mars might get there sooner, once she found that he was rocketing home. He had to make it in two hours this time, and it would be a night landing in a full atmosphere, which was always tricky.

He set his course to bring them in before the two hours were up. It was no time for anything but speed, and the ship could really put out the gees when she was pressed!

Dick came in and started to say something. He was hunched from the weight of the rocket thrust, and he stared at Jerry as if the boy were a madman.

He dropped into the other seat, sighing as the gravity crush was eased from his legs. "You'll make it, kid. You're the sort who does—crazy, maybe, but you get things done. I guess I know what Tod meant, and he was right. We're built to a different size, all around. I've got another job, Jerry."

"You told me about it," Jerry cut in. "Yeah, we're different. I'll probably wind up as some third assistant navigator, and you'll be top engineer in a few years. But just between us, I like it this way."

Dick pulled out a cigarette and began puffing at it. "So do I, kid, now that I'm used to the idea. I've never really been cut out for space—not this end of it. I want to see men go on out. There's Pluto out there, the greatest super-cold laboratory in the world—only a couple of degrees above absolute zero. And with the right fuels, we can get there. I want to help make those fuels. And maybe, if I'm lucky, I'll live to see a ship take off for the stars."

The radar screen emitted a pip of light, and something streaked by overhead. Mars was now in front, her great wash of flame shooting out a bright red toward the Earth below. Jerry watched it, and he swallowed slowly.

"I guess I misunderstood, Dick," he said at last.

Some of the coldness melted. Dick wasn't letting anyone down, after all. He'd be doing something that *really* counted. And maybe Jerry could get a job on that first trip to Pluto—maybe Dick would put in a good word to have him in that group.

He grinned to himself. He'd been a fool again, thinking Dick was interested only in money and easy living. He should have known better.

"Scram, Dick," he ordered. "I can't talk now, and if you stick around, I will talk. But I'm tickled pink about your job."

He felt the big man's hand on his shoulder as he bent over his calculator, estimating the Martian ship's progress. At this distance, they must be making a speed of . . . um-m . . .

It worked out well enough for their 11:15 deadline. The glance he'd had on the screen and the time it had taken for their flare to disappear, mixed with a dozen other factors that he could only guess were there, without knowing why, all added up to the fact that they'd make it before then.

They'd know about him, by now. They must have heard from their group on Earth, who'd send them a message through the Commission, telling all about his leaving the Moon. And it was too close for Mars not to gamble a bit on their tubes holding now.

Unless he had guessed their minds wrong, they would be down on the field by eleven. He'd have to make better time than that.

He no longer questioned the fact that he was going to win. Dick might work his way up in time, even if they lost. They'd prove the value of his father's fuel somehow, though it might take longer, and they'd use that as a basis for even better fuels. It was only the beginning of the low-heat, high-energy breakdown liquids. But if he lost, they'd never believe that it was a leak in the tanks plus inadequate emergency fueling on Venus that had made him drop to the Moon before coming down. And that might slow Dick down for years.

If he won, they'd begin with this fuel at once. With that as a bargaining wedge, Dick could practically control Sun Fuels in five years—and Sun Fuels would have the edge throughout the system.

He grinned to himself. When Dick made his second million, the first thing he would have to buy was a bigger model of the *Last Hope* for his younger brother and Tod. There'd be another Classic in ten years, and he meant to be ready for it, to show them a real pair of heels.

They reached turnover point, according to Jerry's calculations. He stared at the big control that was jammed all the way down, and then at the clock.

Tod was bringing coffee, but he refused it. "Turnover time, Tod," he said.

Tod nodded. "Yep."

"Aren't you going to call me a blamed fool? We can't brake any faster than we're accelerating, and this is the halfway mark."

"Nope—I'm tired of calling you a fool," Tod told him. "I figure I know what you're going to try."

Jerry sat watching the clock for a few minutes more. Then, reluctantly, he hit the steering rockets, and began a flip-over. For the second time, he made an exact counterblast with the first try, to bring the *Last Hope* into blasting position against Earth.

Mars wasn't going to win, even if he had to drive the *Last Hope* through America and halfway to China!

He made sure that the blast was at its maximum again, and watched the clouds and the dim outlines of the continents creep up.

"You're a fool, Tod," he said at last. "A dadblamed fool. If you know what I'm doing, why aren't you telling me off?"

The old man chuckled. "I found out I was a fool a long time ago, boy. But lately, I ain't so sure about it. Lately I'm beginning to think I'm getting my senses. And you don't need to go trying to rile me up by calling me my own names back. Used to be able to when you were a kid, but you're growing up now—and maybe I'm doing the same. We gonna win?"

"We're gonna win!"

"That's what I thought." The engineer lifted his coffee and studied the tele-panel. "And if we don't, well, I was born down there, though I don't remember much except growing up in deep space. But I guess the place where I came into the world's as good a place to go out as any."

He sat in silence for a while longer. Then he stood up slowly. "Like I told Dick, you're a bigger man right now than he ever was. He ain't in your size, kid. Because you're too big a blamed fool to know that you can't beat Mars now, no matter what you do. That's why I ain't worried. I only worry when there are sensible men running these contraptions."

For the second time that night, Jerry felt a hand catch his shoulder and then heard steps moving away. He swallowed softly, and began planning his landing for the fiftieth time."

CHAPTER 18 /

The Checkered Flag

EARTH telescopes must have picked up his flare, and that of the Mars ship. They had good plotters down there, machines and men who could tell to the fraction of a second when and where a ship would touch the atmosphere.

The radio began buzzing almost as soon as Tod left, and Jerry answered it automatically.

"Blaine! You're coming down too fast, and you're going to wind up in the ocean! Put on more power and straighten out."

"Can't," Jerry answered truthfully. "I'm using full power now!"

"Then sheer off and go on. We'll send a tug up to haul you in or refuel you, if you need help. There's no sense in getting yourself killed."

"Just make sure the field is clear for me," Jerry told them, and cut off. The radio went on buzzing, but he refused to answer it. Their hysteria was strong enough that it might affect him, and he had to keep his head clear.

He watched the atmosphere spread out as he drew nearer, and this time when the pip showed on the radar screen, he was passing the Mars ship.

He waited until the last minute, and then hit the steering controls with his feet, while his hands found the little levers that would work the big vanes along the rocket tube.

The *Last Hope* began to come into proper position, and he cut down the thrust of the tube. This time, he yelled a warning to Tod and Dick, and buckled on his safety harness carefully. He was learning finally that it is all the little things that go together to make the big thing that counts. He could keep part of his mind on his job, and send the other thoughts searching for any overlooked details. But none seemed to be overlooked, so far as he could tell.

The first faint whisper of a sound struck his ears from the hull, and there was a touch of resistance to the vane levers. He heard the vane control motors grumbling, and nodded in satisfaction.

He was better prepared in some ways than before, but his choice of angle wasn't as good as it had been on Jupiter; it couldn't be, if he were to reach the port. He began to ease the ship into a glide, using both vanes and steering tubes. When he could, he cut on the big rocket for a moment.

The air outside was whining shrilly now. It wasn't going to be easy. There would be no chance to pull out and go on, as there had been on the big planet. One way or another, his course was downward, but in as flat a glide as he could manage without overshooting the landing field.

His eyes watched the hull pyrometers for signs of overheating, but he wasn't too worried about that. He'd seen what real heat could be, and the ship had taken it.

The ship was fighting the air now, and the heat was piling up. The vanes threatened to pull off under the force he was using, but he could feel the big ship beginning to flatten. The force of the change hit him with more gees than he had felt before, but the harness cushioned some of that.

He was flattening out, though he was already deeper in the atmosphere than was entirely safe. The temperature kept rising, and he could barely avoid blacking out under the pressure. He managed to hold his level, somehow; the resistance of the air was slowing him rapidly, so that he could risk the denser atmosphere. He let the ship drop another few degrees.

Then suddenly it was all over—the screaming sounds went on, but at a lower pitch, and the pyrometer needles stayed where they were, showing that he had nothing to fear from heat. Now it was only a matter of holding the long, steep glide that would let him drop just fast enough so that the denser air matched his lower speed.

Such landings would never be easy—they could never be anything but a dire emergency measure. But he guessed that handling a braking orbit would eventually be part of the training of every young pilot. He could almost feel sorry for those students—except that it would be worth it all, to know how to handle such emergencies.

The Earth-formations were slipping by under him now, but he was dropping more steadily. He waited until he knew the field was below him, then flipped the ship carefully up on its tail and began coming down on the rockets.

The field was blazing with lights, of course. He'd expected that, since he'd seen pictures of one of the old winners who'd come down at night. But for a moment it was blinding.

Then the rays of lights were over him. The field came up steadily. Below him was the rocket pit from which he had taken off. The exhaust touched it now, forming a cushion under him. He set the ship down into the pit softly, cutting off the big tube just as she touched.

The clock showed 10:56. He'd beaten the Martians, and he had set a new record for the race.

Jerry waited until Tod and Dick were beside him before he threw open the big air lock and tossed out the landing ramp to the edge of the pit. There was a noise in the air that kept him from hearing the words they were saying. He finally recognized the sound as the cheers of the crowd. Across the field, held well away from the landing pits by Commission Police, people seemed to be jammed into a solid, cheering mass.

Jerry put his foot over the side of the port, and then drew it back quickly. The hull was still hot. He saw now why no one had come too close.

But the official welcoming committee was waiting, just beyond the pit, motioning him out. They were mounted on a big platform behind the most monstrous tractor he had ever seen, and there were five of them, with other men busily handling television cameras. Jerry groaned to himself and jumped down the ramp toward them, too quickly for the heat of the hull to harm him.

The Commissioner from Earth took his papers and signed them with a flourish. The World Chairman gave him the little piece of ribbon with a dangling bit of metal attached that told him he had officially won first place. The reigning queen of television kissed him soundly on the mouth. He didn't blush, though someone with a bright red light made it seem that way. He wasn't more than half-aware that she was there.

Dick was shaking hands with the President of Sun Fuels, and he seemed to have that one member of the welcoming committee firmly in hand.

The fifth one was Commodore Tenn, head of the Space Institute, and it was on him that Jerry's eyes were fixed. He had a sinking sensation in his stomach. If the man began telling how good he'd always known Jerry was . . .

Tenn moved forward slowly, a heavy man with a solid military bearing, but the smile on his face seemed genuine.

"Hello, Jerry," he said, while the big public address

system carried his words back to the crowd. "I guess I can't ask you to come back to the Institute, though we'd like to have you with us next semester. That would be a little silly, though, since we've just granted you your final degree. You're now Captain Gerald Blaine, Master Navigator, Master Pilot. You proved you deserved the titles."

He paused, and Jerry tried to tell him that he would be back, in spite of his sudden graduation. He'd learned the need for theory, as well as for practice, and one more year of study would help him with the work he wanted to do. But the words seemed to stick in his throat.

Tenn smiled, as if he understood. "You know, Jerry, when I kicked you out for what I thought were good reasons, I told you it took a man to be a good pilot. All I can say now is that I didn't know a good man when I saw one, by Harry! Shake?"

Jerry shook, with more feeling than he'd expected.

It was at that moment that the ship from Mars set down. Jerry tried to climb from the platform, but the Sun Fuels man was holding him back.

He tried to shake the man off, but it was no use. "Just confirmation," the corporation president was asking against his ear, over the thunder of the landing rocket. "Your brother says you own one half of the rights to the fuel. Are you willing to let him speak for you—we'll make it official later, but I want a go-ahead now."

"What he says is fine with me," Jerry assured him. Again he tried to climb down, and this time Commodore Tenn's heavy arm came out to help him over the tangle of television cables.

The Martian ship was down with its port open, and the crew of three were already heading for his ship when he touched the ground. They seemed to be lost on the big field, and there was only a weak and scattered cheer from the crowd for them. Jerry waved to them, and they stopped near the ship, waiting uncertainly.

He started toward them. The Martians were dark, and covered with leather, as all the other Martians had been, though Jerry had never seen these three before. Their faces were composed and stern as they waited for him to reach them.

Then the captain smiled, as much as any Martian ever did. "Jerry Blaine," he said, "that landing was the dirtiest trick to pull on a poor unsuspecting Martian that I can think of. But it does a man's heart good to see an Earthman who knows how to fight—and to win. We've got a bottle or two of zesto on board, if you aren't too proud to visit a second-placing ship."

"Wait a minute," Jerry told him. He swung back, his eyes searching for Tod. The old man was still in the air lock of the *Last Hope,* apparently forgotten. But his head came up quickly when he saw Jerry motion to him, and his old legs carried him toward the boy at a brisk trot.

By tradition, tonight was Jerry's to do with as he wanted, and the crowd wouldn't be allowed to mob him as they had done in earlier days. After the first night, there'd be a few weeks of tortured tours and ridiculous speeches, until his fame wore thin enough for him to go back to school or to be an honest pilot again. But now there would be no objection raised, no matter what he did.

It wouldn't do the inhabited planets any harm to see that men could learn to fight by any means they had for what they believed in, without having to hate each other. There was no place he wanted to be more than on the Martian ship.

He threw his arm over Tod's shoulder and nodded to the Martians. Zesto sounded like a fine idea.

About the Author

Lester del Rey was born in a small farming community of Minnesota in 1915. In 1931, he moved to Washington, D. C., to attend college, but dropped out after two years to work at a series of assorted jobs.

Reading and science were always his main interests, and he discovered the works of Burroughs, Wells, and Verne at an early age. After discovering his first science fiction magazine in 1929, he became a fan of that literature. His first story was written in 1937 on a bet to convince a friend that he could get a personal letter instead of a rejection slip from the editor of *Astounding Stories*. To his surprise, he got a check for the story, "The Faithful." Thereafter he continued to write off and on, becoming one of the most popular writers for the magazine. But it wasn't until 1950 that he turned to writing full-time.

His stories have appeared in numerous magazines and anthologies, and he has had over forty novels published, as well as fact books on atomic power, oceanography, photography, rockets, etc. He has also edited several science fiction and fantasy magazines, and is currently fantasy editor for Ballantine Books.

Among his books which he most enjoyed doing were some dozen novels for younger readers. The first of these, *Marooned on Mars*, won the Boys' Clubs of America award in 1953. Several others became Junior Literary Guild selections.

He now lives in New York City with a collection of typewriters which he rebuilds to his own requirements, a number of overflowing bookcases, and his wife, Judy-Lynn del Rey.